# Vlad and Friends

### A Cozy Dracula Series

Book I

Nicole Holland

Copyright © 2025 by Nicole Holland

All rights reserved.

No part of this publication may be reproduced, distributed, or transmitted in any form or by any means, including photocopying, recording, or other electronic or mechanical methods, without the prior written permission of the publisher, except as permitted by U.S. copyright law. For permission requests, contact Nicole Holland at authornicolehol land@gmail.com. No part of this book may be used or reproduced in any manner for the purpose of training artificial intelligence technologies or systems.

ISBN: 979-8-9910698-4-7

Character Art by Oyasumi (@oyasumi912 on TikTok)

First edition 2025

# VLAD AND FRIENDS

## A Cozy Dracula Series

This work of fiction includes content that may not be appropriate for some readers. Content warnings include foul language, sexual activity, blood, mentions of captivity, mentions of torture (not depicted), and panic/anxiety attacks.

Though this story is inspired by Bram Stoker's *Dracula*, it is not a direct interpretation of the novel and therefore does not follow the original storylines, though some characters and locations may be similar.

# VLAD AND FRIENDS

# 1

## Vlad

The ebony clock in the Great Hall struck a singular, resounding gong. Vlad hardly heard it. He was busy planning his next move.

Moonlight poured through the tall arched windows, casting drastic shadows on the marble chess set he'd carved back when crushing isolation and fears of immortality claimed his nightmares.

A long, long time ago.

Silver fingers tapped to the ticking of the clock as he pondered whether to move a bishop or a pawn. The only other sounds in the enormous space were the occasional cracks of logs in the hearth as they shifted. Despite the fire's warmth, the bitterness of winter seeped through the castle walls and nestled in the opulent furniture and ornate rugs. Items once colorful and lively now dulled by disuse and the cold light of the moon.

"Any day now," Balthazar said from his seat atop a stack of velvet pillows. With the fire as their only light source, the two friends sat in flickering orange while the rest of the hall faded into a blackened abyss. Disconcerting for most, though not for those with night vision. One of them cursed with it, the other born attuned to the darkness.

Vlad made a decision but found himself in checkmate within two moves. A frequent outcome, though he wasn't sure how he'd missed such an obvious ploy.

The victor smiled across the table, sharp and toothy. Balthazar nudged the pieces back into a starting position with his slender snout. "You've been distracted as of late. What troubles you, sire?"

Vlad rose and made for the window, sliding both hands into the pockets of his pleated pants. Clouds raced across the sky. Here one moment and gone the next. Wisps that could travel the world.

The monotonous clock ticked on as Vlad stood there watching. All he ever did was watch. He was as stationary as the ink black castle he looked out from. "I must feed."

The words were routine. Emotionless.

"Shall I accompany you?" Balthazar asked.

"No need to trouble yourself. I should like to dine alone."

The bat studied him with pale pink eyes, unlike Vlad's blood-red; neither having a say in how the color was given to them or how they became trapped in a never-ending cycle. Days and nights repeated, so unchanging in their scenery that years passed with painful slowness and growing apathy.

Balthazar squeaked his concern and flew across the room, landing on the count's shoulder.

Vlad scooped a raspberry out of a bowl and fed it to his friend. "I'm fine, Zar. Just one of those nights."

"Even more of a reason to go with you." The bat rode on his shoulder as Vlad removed himself from the Great Hall that had once been filled with merriment. Now, the gray stone walls were ever dark, save for the glow of the hearth or the occasional candle. And the laughter, well...Vlad had not heard the sound in quite some time.

He let his powerful nocturnal eyesight guide him through the dim halls and into the foyer where Balthazar found a new perch. The bat fluttered to his favorite lookout spot hidden in the rib vaulted ceiling that had been erected with more care and love than Vlad's parents had ever shown him.

"I shall await your return, sire," Balthazar said.

Vlad donned his wolf's fur coat and satin top hat. Black leather gloves of the finest quality slid over his large hands, custom made. They cost a handsome sum, but money was no object to the only remaining heir of the late Dracula family's fortune.

"I shan't be gone long." He knew Balthazar saw through the lie, but the bat simply nodded.

Vlad was grateful for his companion. Zar knew when to speak. When the silence in Vlad's ears became so deafening he could hardly stand it. But he also knew when to stifle his concerns.

Vlad Dracula was impenetrable. Immortal. Concern was not for him, for he would always survive it. His curse to remain.

He slipped out a side exit, forgoing the double oak doors in the main entry whose groan hadn't been heard since that awful night when his entire world changed.

Flurries dusted his shoulders and black boots crunched atop inches of snow that had accumulated in a few short hours. The scent of balsam firs growing in thick clusters around the estate welcomed him into the crisp night. As Vlad made the familiar journey into the woods and down the mountain, he wished for an interruption. A great calamity to uproot his life. Something. Anything.

He watched his steps, not in concern for his footing, but because there was nothing new to see. Nothing he hadn't encountered or tried in the one-hundred-and-forty years he'd been without true human companionship. Gardening, sewing, knitting, chess, music, woodworking—he'd done it all. Such was his misfortune to live long enough to experience all life offered, only to not find lasting joy in any of it.

A thickness coalesced in his throat. *Had he ever known joy?*

Vlad sensed an animal nearby. He stopped. Sniffed the air.

*A deer.*

Traveling in a blur of speed, he covered a quarter mile in a blink. Sharp fangs found the animal's neck so quickly the buck didn't have time to bleat. Vlad tried to go for the elder animals or those sick and dying, as their blood tasted the same. He didn't care for unnecessary suffering.

Its body went limp, and he could practically taste the old buck's gratitude in the sweetness of its life source pumping into his body. The ecstasy of the pains of its existence finally being over.

He envied the creature. It had an end and a beginning. He was stuck somewhere in between. After drinking all its blood, Vlad slung the buck around his shoulders with ease and carried it down the steep terrain.

When he made it to the designated spot sequestered in the trees, halfway between his castle and the village of Newthorn two miles below, Vlad dropped the deer by the stone marker. The humans would fetch their meal come dawn, though he suspected they would arrive much later due to the revelry occurring in the valley.

Each hut glowed from within, and the fire in the village center raged as the celebration burned the night orange. Dancing silhouettes surely lost to the drink moved fluidly in their carefree state.

Less than sixty small homes scattered the valley. Single dwellings on the outskirts with groups of homes surrounding the larger buildings in the main section of the village. To the east—a church, a graveyard, and a stable. Each belonging to Vlad's own estate yet no longer used or visited. Pieces of his home left to decay without the people or the care to maintain it.

He took a seat on a fallen log, shielding himself from the snowfall under the limbs of a massive fir. No music could be heard, so Vlad hummed a tune from his youth. A lively jig his mother had taught him years before she'd given her only son to the witch who cursed him with his affliction.

The mental cage he'd been trapped in during his time in the witch's captivity was returning with haste as moments of panic grew more frequent. Nights waking up in cold sweats and the inability to calm his mind riddled the count with anxiety. Unsure how to stop it and unable to wrangle his emotions in those moments expanded the hollow emptiness inside Vlad's half-beating heart.

He would have to learn to live with his panic. There was no other choice.

The shadowy dancers below continued indulging in the festivities, and Vlad wondered if anyone in Newthorn ever felt like he did, or if he was utterly alone in his torment.

The celebration would last into the late hours, but his offering would freeze overnight and not go to waste. Long ago, he'd coordinated the exchange with the elders whose time on earth had certainly come by now. The deal was one large animal a night in exchange for the villagers leaving Vlad and his home alone. No more breaking through the iron gates and trying to burn the castle down. No more banging on the doors to see if there truly was a "monster" living inside.

Though, as time dragged on, Vlad sometimes wished for the angry mob to return. Anything to put some excitement into his life. Even if their goal was his death.

He wasn't sure how long he sat there watching. Mind emptying of any hope of ever being part of a community again as he hummed song after song.

Once the humans retrieved the deer, they'd return to their lives full of friendship, family, and love.

His heart lurched. He knew friendship, but what must it be like to know love?

An owl hooted, signaling the peak of night. Time to go home. Balthazar would soon be worried.

# 2

## Lenore

All of the men in Newthorn were lousy, incapable idiots. Lenore had known this for years, but today her father had proven himself to be a moron of the highest class.

"I told you winter would start early, father. The trees don't lie." The folded leaves of a merange tree slipped through her calloused fingers, a sign of even colder weather to come.

Her father rubbed his temples. He'd gotten deep into the bottle at the celebration the night prior and she could smell the ale wafting from his breath.

Lenore hadn't bothered with the festivities. She was busy solidifying her escape plan instead.

"Stick to what you know, child," he grumbled.

"I am a woman of twenty-six years, not some ill-mannered pup."

"Ha! You are the definition of ill-mannered. Now go where you are useful. The children need tending."

"This farm needs proper tending..."

"What was that?" Her father leaned on a spade that could hardly break ground. Ignoring her advice to wait to harvest, he'd prematurely dug up the potatoes with great difficulty, cursing at their coin-like size.

Lenore dropped the bucket of pathetic vegetables and stomped through the snow. Most mornings started with an argument between them and today was no different. Reconciliation was inconceivable with a man as stubborn as Remus, no matter how many times she tried. She yanked on the door to their hut and wished for the hinges to snap just so she could refuse to fix it and he would actually have to do something useful.

It didn't take long to march into her room, as their entire home could be cleared in a matter of seconds. Lenore grabbed a pack out from under her lumpy mattress, not bothering to stuff the straw falling out of a tear in the linen back inside.

She would leave tonight. Shademoss was a three day's ride and soon she could start over in a new place with more people.

"I'm going somewhere where they appreciate a woman's ideas." She wadded up a floor-length skirt and two blouses, shoving them into the pack, adding a coin purse that included her final payment from cleaning dishes at the inn, along with money from a few farm jobs she'd done for some of the elders who could no longer work the land.

With a body built for hard labor, her strong muscles were an asset, but Lenore wanted more than a life of farming and animal husbandry. She wanted adventure. Excitement. To follow her passions, whatever they may be. It was pointless to dream in Newthorn, and she wouldn't die in this mud-and-shit-soaked village.

She would have left at that moment, but she volunteered to help watch the community's children. Too many women had died from complications in childbirth though their babies had survived. With the little ones outnumbering the motherly help and Lenore not having any offspring of her own, she assisted in their care when able.

Just a few hours of getting spit up on and keeping the older children corralled, then she'd be gone. Lenore peeked out the window. Her father yelled at Marty who often refused to pull the ploy. When the mule yawned, Remus threw up his hands and cursed at the sky.

She chuckled. Marty may be old, but he was still capable of pulling a cart. She prayed he'd have the stamina to make it up the mountain. Once they passed Castle Dracula, it would be a downhill trek the rest of the way to Shademoss, and all would be well.

As she headed for the building doubling as a weaving room and the children's school, Lenore found her eyes drifting to the midnight-black castle in the distance looming over the valley. Thin, tall turrets like spikes threatened to pierce the clouds and windows that never revealed light darkened the ghoulish monstrosity. Up close, it must be horrific.

Though never seen by anyone still alive, the silver devil rumored to live in the castle was blamed for everything—A missing goat. A lame horse. A poor harvest.

How could a man be capable of such things? Was he even a man? Or was he truly the 'monster on the mountain', as he was called.

She didn't care who he was. The Dracula estate could be abandoned for all anyone knew. No one had ventured there in decades. Some claimed to see a creature stalking through the trees, but the woods between Newthorn and the castle had a way of playing tricks on the eye.

"Something hunts in the night," people would say, gathered around their fires, telling their ghost stories. "Stay clear of the woods, lest you become food for the Devil."

It was all nonsense to Lenore. They were just tales meant to keep children from wandering off and adults from thinking they could ever leave this place.

But she knew better. More importantly, she was not afraid of setting out on her own. With no mother, no siblings, and a father without a loving bone in his body, her absence would hardly be a bother.

The small rotation of lovers would miss her, but none of them provided stimulating conversation or had ambitions of their own. They were clumsy drunks, always fumbling with her ties and content to spend generations in this stifling place.

A few people ambled about the village in the gray morning light doing their chores—hanging clothes on the line, blanketing their donkeys, and pulling fruits off trees that somehow managed to produce in winter. Smoke drifted out of chimneys and the sound of the blacksmith putting hammer to anvil rang out in the bitter air.

Lenore tucked her long blonde hair under a fur-lined hood and pulled the wool coat tighter around her. She hurried to the school before the growing winds had a chance to bite at her skin further.

The shrieks of twenty or so youngsters in the main room stabbed her ears. Mornings were for waking up slowly, but children didn't believe in such things.

"You're here. Finally..." Mary's obvious annoyance was made worse by her shrill voice.

"I said I'd be here within the hour. I'm barely late." Lenore scraped mud off her boots and rubbed her hands together, warming them.

Mary handed her the baby she was holding and sneered at Lenore's dirty skirt. "It's not like you have your own kids to tend to like the rest of us. What could keep you from being here on time?"

*Oh, I don't know. Raising unruly animals. Plowing a frozen field. Working with a useless father.*

"I was busy," Lenore said, "but I'm here now."

Nina avoided looking at them both and made herself busy folding blankets.

"You don't have a husband who needs you at home, so honestly, Lenore, how selfish can you be?"

She didn't bother telling Mary there were other things in life that could take up one's time besides children and a husband. They'd had that argument one too many times. "I wasn't that late."

After the wretched woman left, Nina apologized on her behalf. "Sorry about her."

Lenore rested the baby she'd been given against her shoulder and began burping her. "It's fine. I'm used to it by now."

Nina was one of the few people she would miss. She was kind and far undeserving of the verbal berating from her husband and his constant need to put a child inside her. She wobbled over to the bassinet and set the blankets down, resting a hand on her bloated belly. "Are you okay to take over?" The young woman's eyes were sunken, and Lenore doubted she ever got a moment's peace to sleep.

"I got it." After little Ivy burped her breakfast, Lenore set her in a rickety crib with two other infants.

Nina smiled weakly. "Thank you."

"Before you leave, I have something for you." Lenore unclasped the bracelet around her wrist, grabbed Nina's hand, and placed the jewelry in her palm. It wasn't much. A bit of coiled iron to look like vines, but it was all she could offer. "Happy belated birthday. I'm sorry I forgot."

Nina's dull eyes blew wide. "I...I can't accept this."

"Yes, you can. You deserve it." What she couldn't say was 'this is my parting gift, friend. Good luck to you.'

The woman's bottom lip wobbled, eyes watering as she pulled her in for a hug. "Thank you."

Lenore patted her on the back and watched her only friend waddle to the door, praying for her wellbeing. Nina had plenty of friends here. She was one of those people you could effortlessly get along with. She didn't have a quick temper or the impatience that often got the best of Lenore.

When she was the only adult left in the room, Lenore faced the gaggle of tiny faces, hands on her hips. "Well, little munchkins. What shall we do on our last day together?"

# VLAD AND FRIENDS

After the children had all been retrieved by their mothers, Lenore headed home. She would cook dinner and wait until Remus drank himself into oblivion before heading out. When she opened the door, she found her father snoring in the light of a stubby candle, a bottle of some foul-smelling ale in his hand.

Perfect. He'd already done the work.

She placed the loaf of bread and carrots acquired on the way home in a basket, lit a candle, and quietly carried it into her room. The sun was minutes from setting and soon she could make her escape. After checking that Remus was truly asleep and pacing her room with both nerves and elation, Lenore slung the pack she'd stashed over her shoulder. She retrieved the basket of food from the kitchen and slunk toward the front door.

Lenore paused. It wasn't her father's fault that age had crippled his leg or that her mother had passed when she was young and sent him in to despair. But it was his fault that he blamed Lenore for all of it.

He couldn't take accountability, and she'd tried to be the daughter he wanted, but nothing she ever did was right. So Lenore learned to work on her own and weather the complaints, even though the reason they had food and shelter was because of her.

She squeezed her eyes shut. *Was it wrong to leave her father to fend for himself knowing he would likely fail?*

"You can't let his faults control your life," Nina had once told her. "He doesn't get to dictate your worth."

She'd tried, but over the years her patience with him waned until it no longer existed. You could only help someone so much until they had to help themselves.

Others in the village would help Remus carry on. She wouldn't leave him to die, but Lenore refused to let him keep her down. She had dreams and ambitions, and unlike most in Newthorn, she *believed* she could achieve them.

A solemn, "Goodbye, father," slipped out of her mouth. Nothing more. Nothing less. An apt farewell.

With as much stealth as she could muster, Lenore hooked Marty up to the cart under the cover of darkness. A blanket covered her pack, basket of food, and a few other items in the back.

When she was through, Lenore climbed into the seat and gathered the reins. A lantern rode next to her, along with a waterskin and a sack of grain she'd almost forgotten. Thankfully, the wind had died down and it hadn't snowed all day. Hopefully the dirt road up the mountain would be fairly easy to traverse. She made sure no one was around before softly clucking to Marty.

The mule plodded along the outskirts of the village. Each loud dip of the cart in a hole had Lenore wincing, praying no one would step outside and see who was making such a ruckus.

When she finally cleared Newthorn and began the climb up the mountain, Lenore let out a wild cackle.

"I'm free! Finally, God-damned free! I can't believe it."

She leaned back in the seat and watched the clouds effortlessly slide past the moon. The night was peaceful. Calm. The wind gone and the chill more bearable than it'd been in days. The promising air invigorated Lenore as visions of a new life ran through her mind like wildfire.

Starting a flower shop. Working in a smithy. Training horses. Buying a cottage by the river. She could do anything. For the first time, she had options. Possibilities. Hope.

After two hours or so, Marty began wheezing. Lenore pulled him off the path and guided him a short distance into the woods. They'd gone far enough for tonight. Once she'd unhooked him from the cart and tied the mule to a tree with enough slack to graze, Lenore made quick work of setting up a makeshift bed in the back of the cart. The bundle of wool layers kept her warm enough, and after pulling a tarp over the cart to keep any overnight snow out, she curled into a ball.

The sounds of crickets and Marty chewing lulled her to sleep. She did not fear the creature of the night rumored to be lurking in these woods. The 'monster on the mountain' was a ghost story, and Lenore had stopped believing in those long ago.

# 3

## Lenore

Marty proved to be slower than she'd thought. Almost a full day passed and they still hadn't crested the mountain. With the bread and apple she'd had for breakfast wearing thin, the quick annoyance that accompanied hunger struck. Lenore found multiple outlets for her frustrations. Blaming her father. Marty. The terrain. She'd reined it in by dusk, but when one of the axles broke, Lenore erupted.

"Stupid piece of shit!" She hopped off the cart and kicked the wobbly wheel, instantly regretting it, cradling her throbbing toes and yelling, "God-damnit! We're never going to get there!"

Marty yawned.

She groaned up at the bleeding sky. Night would arrive quickly, and the sinister color of the clouds signaled more misfortune if she didn't take shelter soon.

After a few more huffs and puffs, Lenore set her hands on her hips and surveyed the situation. They had to be close to the top of the mountain by now, but the firs bordering the road were too lofty to discern much. She left Marty with the cart and entered the woods, finding a small clearing that provided a glimpse of dark spires a short distance ahead. She calculated they couldn't be more than a half mile from Castle Dracula.

A curiosity struck.

If the castle was abandoned, she could take shelter inside and allow Marty a night of rest. Surely an estate belonging to a once illustrious family had stables. But if the castle wasn't abandoned...

"It's a ghost story, you fool. Go now, before the cold gets you both." Lenore took what food she could carry and tied her pack to Marty's harness, draping the blankets and tarp over his back.

She grumbled a few curse words when snow started falling, wishing for a break in the weather that wouldn't come anytime soon. Leading the mule on foot, she donned her hood and clutched her coat with numb fingers, forming a plan.

There wasn't another shelter for miles, and Shademoss was still a day and a half away, so she would stall Marty in the stables, get a good night's sleep, then scour the castle in the morning for any tools to repair the axle.

The campfire tales she'd heard all her life came rushing back. At the height of the sixteenth century, a strange illness swept through the castle during a royal ball, killing everyone inside. 'Piles of bodies. Veins gone black,' went the stories. 'But when we returned the next day to remove them, they were gone. No people. No blood. No nothing.'

Townsfolk promptly started taking everything of value, only to be interrupted by 'a red-eyed, silver-skinned demon.' The thieves fled in sheer terror and the tales of Castle Dracula amplified over the years.

Some held steadfast it was a possessed child they saw. Others remained convinced only a man of great strength was capable of such a travesty. Whatever the case, only a curious few ventured back, but eventually, people stopped trying to gain access. Rumors festered—as they often do between idle folk—of the castle being occupied by the silver demon, though Lenore doubted there was much truth to it.

*Who would choose to live alone in such a dreary place?*

Almost an hour later, she made it to a flat outcropping, legs burning from the vertical climb. Marty wheezed along with her.

"No wonder people stopped coming up here." Puffs of frozen air accompanied her laborious breathing, but relief was just up ahead. Set off the main road, a black, wrought iron fence with arrow-tipped rods ran the length of the estate it guarded.

A masterful piece of Gothic architecture sat undisturbed in the middle of the grounds. She counted four stories, but its height was almost too tall to fathom. The knobs on the spires were so plentiful she couldn't count them all. Gigantic lanterns built into the entry were unlit, their glass frozen and pale with frost. No light came from inside the multi-paned, arched windows and the chimney didn't puff smoke. Not a single footprint led up the wide set of stairs to the double doors.

Surely no-one lived in such an inhospitable home.

As she neared the main gates, the wind stopped abruptly like the extinguishing of a candle. The world went still. Not a single animal could be heard, only the soft landing of snowfall as fat flurries whitened the landscape.

She paused, scanning the area. A prickling started on her scalp.

"It's okay. Nothing's out here," Lenore repeated until she half-believed it. She tugged on Marty's reins, but the mule planted his feet. His head shot up, ears pointed forward and nostrils flared.

She surveyed the area again. No movement. The trees stood like frozen sentries guarding the forest. Watching her. Daring her to continue.

The silence was so eerie Lenore could hear her heartbeat thump in her ears. After a few words of encouragement, Marty apprehensively started walking. She led him closer to the entrance—two large iron gates with a giant, swirling letter "D" cutting both gates in half. She noticed a slight gap between the halves.

It was open.

Before entering, Lenore walked down the fence line bordering the estate. Further down, stables with shut windows and part of the roof sloping sat off to the side. Toward the back of the home, a chapel with stained glass windows brought the only color to the otherwise lifeless surroundings. Headstones dotted the east side of the church, some leaning in macabre directions and broken in places.

Lenore took her time walking back to the entrance, using the delay as an excuse to dig up her courage. "Just a ghost story. That's all it is." After a few more minutes of consideration, staring at the castle and scanning the woods again, she made her decision.

The gates balked under pressure; creaking like they hadn't moved since that fateful day. Her farming muscles forced the left side open until there was enough room to pass through.

She crossed the yard with a tight grip on Marty's lead, listening for any signs of life, but even the birds remained quiet. Old wagons sat untouched, wooden barrels were split and broken, and weeds sprouted out of the snow in old flowerbeds.

The stables were in fairly good shape, considering. Only a few dilapidated boards, but it was warmer inside. She led Marty into one of the many stalls and turned a feed bucket over, shaking out the dust and brushing off spiderwebs. Water from a second waterskin she'd brought specifically for him went into the old bucket, and while Marty drank deeply, Lenore filled a smaller bucket with a third of the bag of grain. She searched the tack room and hay loft for any grain or hay, not surprised when she didn't find any. After removing the mule's harness and untying her belongings from his tack, Lenore patted him on the neck. "I'll come back after I check out the castle and see if I can find a place for you to graze."

She grabbed the pack, blankets, and her waterskin before shutting him in.

Castle Dracula was daunting from the road, but up close, it was quite beautiful. Intricate floral carvings, circular rose windows, pointed arches, and swooping buttresses in layers of black stone made for a magnificent creation that must have taken years to erect. She wondered if the inside was just as elaborate.

As Lenore drew nearer to the front doors made of dark-stained oak with a dragon's maw for handles, her heart quickened.

What if the demon *was* inside?

"Don't be ridiculous," she muttered, though she couldn't stop her hands from trembling. And it wasn't from the cold.

Palming a small knife she'd tucked into her boot, Lenore crept up the steps. A near-useless weapon against a monster, but it was all she had.

The iron handle burned from the cold through her gloves, and when she pulled, the door didn't budge. She tried pushing but was met with the same resistance. Lenore leaned a shoulder into the door and pushed harder. Grunting her exertion did nothing as her boots slid across the snow-covered stones.

Determined, she took a moment to collect herself. The knife went back into her boot as she took a deep breath, squatted down, and threw all her weight against the wood.

Suddenly, the resistance was removed and the door flew open.

She fell face first, her belongings spewing across the ground. One of her apples rolled across the marble, and when it stopped at the toe of a black boot, Lenore slowly looked up and screamed.

# 4

## Lenore

Forgetting her knife, Lenore jumped up and grabbed the closest item she could find. An unlit candelabra.

Holding the pronged object out in front of her, she waited for her eyes to adjust to the darkness. After a few rapid blinks, she could make out a staircase and a silver-skinned shadow standing in front of it.

"Stay back!"

The monster stared at her with piercing ruby eyes. "Are you real?"

The voice that came out of him was certainly human, but his seven-foot height was not. Black and white formal wear from another time period clung to his large frame, and short raven hair was brushed back from his sculpted face. He was a marble statue disguised as a human. A devil taking on the form of something he once was.

She trembled. "You—"

"Why are you here?" he asked, unmoving.

"Are you...the monster?"

Thick, black brows scrunched and the lines in his forehead deepened.

She took a step back.

A muscle in his clean-shaven jaw clenched. "I am not a monster."

Careful not to offend further, she went with a neutral word. "Are you the legend of this castle?"

The long line of his broad shoulders relaxed slightly. "My name is Vlad, and this is my home."

He *was* real.

"Vlad Dracula," she whispered in astonishment. "The last heir."

He smiled, and it was shockingly beautiful. When his pointed canines showed, warning bells went off in her head.

'Feasted like an animal.'

'A beast-man.'

'Savage.'

Lenore dropped the candelabra and ran for the exit.

In a speed too fast for any human to move, he reached over her and pushed the door shut. "Wait!"

She screamed and ducked under his arm, quickly putting distance between them.

"Just listen," he said, massive hands raised.

She backed away, breaths coming faster. "You can't keep me here! I'll—I'll run away! I'll find a way to escape!"

"I promise I'm not going to hurt you."

The closer he got, the more their height difference frightened her. He could crush her skull with a squeeze of his hand and use her brains to decorate the walls.

Lenore glanced at the staircase and made a run for it. She flew up the steps and bolted down a long hallway. The red sky outside the series of windows, the dark painted halls, and the lack of candlelight increased her panic. She rounded a corner and spared a glance over her shoulder.

Alone.

Lenore turned the handle of the next door she came upon, grateful it was unlocked. She pressed her body to the wood and flipped the lock, releasing a shaky but relieved breath.

After waiting for minutes and not hearing any footsteps, she turned and took in the room. Minimal light from the triple windows illuminated the silhouette of a bed against the far wall with other large objects of differing sizes covered in sheets.

Patterns in the carpet swirled in various colors, more decorative than anything she'd ever laid eyes on. Nothing like the vomit green, threadbare rug in her old room.

Fumbling through the desk for matches proved fruitful. Lenore lit a candelabra and let the light guide her around the room. Curious, she pulled back the sheet to the closest piece of furniture, gasping at the amount of gold trim on the chaise and wondering what price such an item could fetch. Enough to feed her entire village for a month, at least.

"Miss?"

The voice that spoke from the other side of the door was softer. Lighter.

She kept rooted to her spot. "Who is it?"

"My name is Balthazar. I can offer some explanation about what occurred downstairs, if you'll grant me entrance."

Whispers sounded in the hall. Two voices.

Lenore crept across the room and pressed her ear to the door.

"Ask her what her name is," a deep, hushed voice asked. *The monster.* "Ask her to come out."

"I can't do that yet. She's frightened," the softer voice whispered. "Miss, if you would permit me entrance, I will answer all of your questions."

"Who are you? Are you...like him?" She didn't know the word for it.

Silence. Then more whispering. Indistinguishable.

"I am only here to make you understand, miss. I will not cause you harm. On my honor."

"That's good," the deep voice said, upbeat and excited. "Very reassuring."

She chewed on the inside of her cheek. Lenore had some heft to her, and she'd wrestled many an uncooperative sheep in her time, so she could handle the smaller man if it came to it, but not the monster. "How do I know he won't push through the door if I let you in?"

"I would never!"

A smacking sound rang out.

"Ow," the monster said like he'd been scolded.

"I am not here to deceive you, miss. Only I will enter."

Lenore wasn't a fool. She wouldn't have her only exit blocked by two men. "No," she said firmly.

Grumbles sounded as the men engaged in some kind of debate. The voices stopped, and the longer the silence dragged on, the more nervous she became.

Lenore was about to call out when something rapped on the window.

A bat hovered outside, wearing what looked like a men's white dress shirt collar around his neck. She had to blink twice to make sure she was seeing it correctly.

"Now will you let me in? It's freezing out here."

The bat's mouth moved, but she couldn't believe it was…talking.

"*You're* Balthazar? You speak?"

"It would seem so."

Better odds to fight off a rotund little bat than a massive devil. Lenore chuckled at the absurdity of the image. She cranked the handle to the window and the bat slipped in, perching on the back of a covered chair. He sat like a bird and not on all fours like a bat should.

She couldn't make sense of it.

He bat shook off flurries from his gray fur. "It's dreadful out there. Nasty business, this early winter." Charcoal colored wings stretched, barely reaching two feet in length. His round, furry body was no bigger than the size of her hand, but it was his pink eyes that interested her most. She'd never seen a bat with pink eyes. Or one that could talk.

"I can't believe I'm speaking to a bat."

Balthazar huffed like he was offended. "I am so much more than my species. As evident by my prolific vocabulary and exquisite taste in well, everything." He lifted his tiny snout, showing off the fabric around his neck.

"Well, you're certainly full of yourself, at the very least. And am I hallucinating, or is that a collar made from a dress shirt?"

"I am most dignified, so one should dress as such. And might I remind you, you are a guest in this house and should conduct yourself with respect for those who live here."

"I do not intend to stay."

"Is that why you're hiding in a bedroom then?" The creature smirked.

Lenore crossed her arms, frowning. "Look, I'm traveling to Shademoss and my cart broke about a mile down the mountain, so I brought my mule and put him in the stables. I was just planning on resting here for the night, then repairing the cart in the morning and going about my way."

"So you assumed you would be welcome in a place where you trespassed?" Balthazar tsked.

"Many people thought this place was abandoned. Including me."

He cocked his head. "What do you mean? The count has dealings with both Shademoss and Newthorn. Everyone knows the castle is occupied."

She gaped. "What do you mean he has *dealings* with Newthorn?"

Balthazar's pink eyes darted around. "It is not my place to speak on such things."

Lenore drew nearer. "Yes, it is. You said you would answer all my questions."

"I am the count's esteemed council. Do not think you are in a position to demand anything from me."

She laughed. "You are a bat!"

Balthazar tsked again, shaking his head. "So much physical beauty but so small-minded. Such a pity."

Lenore grabbed a pillow off the bed and threw it at him.

He dodged it with ease. "When you're done acting like a petulant child, let me know so I can escort you to the Great Hall." Balthazar flew to the door and used his weight to flip the lock, impressively opening it and flying into the hall.

Lenore pressed her fingers to her temples. *Was she going insane? Was she really about to follow the orders of a talking bat?"*

The gloves went into her skirt pocket as she trailed after him.

"Keep close," Balthazar said. "And do try not to get the mud from your boots all over everything like you did those beautiful carpets in there."

She rolled her eyes. *Condescending little mammal.*

As she followed her self-absorbed guide, Lenore admired the portraits on the walls, each of someone dressed in finery from another era and hair in styles no longer worn.

"Are all of these portraits of the Dracula family?" she asked.

"The count shall tell you the details of his home, if he so wishes."

"I thought you said you'd answer my questions? You haven't done a very good job of it so far."

Balthazar eyed her over his shoulder. Did bats have shoulders? Perhaps it was just called a wing. Distracted by his anatomy, Lenore knocked into a painting.

"Do watch where you step," he snapped.

She stared at the picture of a man and a woman each wearing a crown, resting their hands on the shoulder of a young boy with ink-black hair, brown eyes, and a proud smile.

A smile before it had two sharp fangs.

"Come along, miss." Balthazar flitted down the stairs, Lenore following him down to the first floor. The cool air smelled faintly of neglect, neither sweet nor musty. Stagnant. Stuck.

They passed under a high arch framed by two unused sconces. The candles inside had most of their height and cobwebs hung about the casing.

Lenore froze when she stepped into the Great Hall. A line of unlit chandeliers started above her and stretched all the way to the end of the room that seemed to go on forever. Dust covered the crystals and barely reflected the glow from the only light source—a wide-mouthed hearth burning in full.

She tore herself from admiration and called out to Balthazar, "My mule. Do you have anything I can feed him? Or fresh water?"

"I shall ask the count." The bat slipped through a side door, and Lenore had the good sense not to follow.

Black velvet curtains covered every east and west facing window. The furniture was trimmed in gold like the chaise in the bedroom and patterned in multiple colors. Rugs covered nearly all of the stone floors, fringed on the ends and vibrant against the otherwise dreary colors.

Set in front of the fire was a well-loved, leather chair and a matching one across it with pillows stacked to the height of the table. A marble chess set appearing mid-game occupied the space between them.

Lenore trailed her fingers over the board, careful not to disturb the pieces. The empty chair beckoned her, and when she sat down, the seat welcomed her like a pair of warm arms. A hearty scent enveloped her senses. The smell of trees after a rainstorm, woodsy and smokey from the fire at her side.

Apprehension fell by the wayside as she sank into the leather, watching the logs burn. Apparently even monsters enjoyed human comforts.

# 5

# VLAD

Vlad plastered his face to the small window in the door. His breath fogged up the glass. "Look at her, Balthazar. I must go talk to her."

The woman sat in his chair, tapping her fingers on the armrest and staring at the hearth. Every fiber of Vlad's being wanted to burst into the room.

"She is quite obstinate, sire."

"You talked to her for five minutes. That's not long enough to know her."

Balthazar shifted on a chair back. "She showed me enough of her character."

"This is the first time anyone's come here in decades, Zar. And last time it was to try and burn this place down."

"Those human morons back then didn't know stone doesn't burn."

The bat chuckled and Vlad glared at him. "I was human once."

Balthazar shrank. "I apologize, sire. I'm only trying to look out for you. She said she was traveling to Shademoss and that her mule is in the stables. I'm not sure if I believe her. Could be a ploy to try and do you harm."

Vlad glanced at the items she'd dropped in the foyer he'd investigated earlier. "She has a pack with clothes, food, and water. I'd say she was being truthful about where she was headed. There was no a torch, only a small lantern. I don't think she came here with ill intent."

He took a moment to study the woman's heart-shaped face and pouty pink lips. Long blonde hair pulled back into two thick braids with frizzy pieces in the front framed her face. His eyes traveled over her ample chest, ignoring her filthy coat and skirt that flared over her wide hips.

Gorgeous.

Vlad was drawn to her physically, but his heart quickened for another reason. "I have not spoken to another person in far too long, Zar. I have a chance here to change the narrative about me." He couldn't bring himself to say the other reason. That he longed so deeply for connection that the dangerous thoughts had been creeping in again. Vlad didn't want to be alone anymore. He wanted a human friend, so he pushed into the room against Balthazar's wishes to wait.

The woman startled.

Vlad paused, lifting his hands, showing her he was no threat.

She gripped the armrests, eyes wide like one crack of a twig would send the fawn scattering.

"I know the stories you've likely heard about me," he said softly. "I just ask that you give me a chance to explain. My friend told me you traveled from Newthorn and that you stalled your mule in my stables."

Balthazar flapped into the room and landed on the chaise.

The woman's jade eyes darted from Zar back to him.

"You are both welcome here. Though I don't have hay, there is grass in my garden I can give to your mule, and you're welcome to the vegetables in my greenhouse. Well, I don't have much, but there are potatoes and carrots and...uhh..."

Vlad rubbed the back of his neck, knowing he was rambling. "What I mean to say is, stay as long as you want. I don't get company often."

*Or ever.*

Her grip on the chair eased. "No, I suppose you don't."

Her voice was the first spring rose to bloom. The shimmer of snow in the setting sun. A church bell to his ears. Vlad's half-dead heart pounded with excitement. He forced himself not to move and accidentally scare her again.

She glanced at Balthazar. "Your pet was quite rude to me."

"I am no one's pet! And one should consider looking in a mirror, miss."

Vlad flashed him a look. "I apologize for my friend's behavior toward you. It has been some time since either of us have conversed with anyone but each other."

Her brows pinched. What was that look? Was it pity? Curiosity? Confusion? Had he forgotten how to read people entirely?

Vlad gestured to the chair across from her. "May I sit?"

She watched him intensely. "I think I'm in your chair."

He lifted a hand as she began to rise. "Please, you may have my seat." Vlad moved Balthazar's pillows and set them on the ground.

The bat glared at them both.

He worked in slow movements to help ease her mind, though her eyes flicked to both exits. Planning her escape, if needed.

Smart, but it still hurt.

Vlad tried to make himself appear less menacing, resting an ankle on his opposite knee and leaning back, but fine clothing couldn't overshadow his fangs or eyes.

The woman watched him warily.

"What is your name?" he asked.

She set her hands in her lap and fidgeted with her long skirt. "Lenore."

A whisper slipped right out of him. "Beautiful."

Her pale cheeks flushed and her eyes flashed downward.

Oh no. *Had he said the wrong thing?*

"It's quite a regal name," he said, trying to recover. "A name meaning 'light'. Like a beacon of hope. A salvation."

She chuckled awkwardly. "I doubt anyone sees me as such."

"Why do you say that?"

*Tell me everything. Let me know you.* Vlad forced himself not to say the words out loud. He needed to slow down, but he couldn't believe he was actually talking to another person. Someone not trying to kill him.

"I doubt those back home would agree," she said. "I didn't even know my name meant that. My father picked it, and he is anything but a 'light'."

"Maybe that's why he chose it for you then. To be his beacon."

She crossed her arms, supple mouth tightening. "Kindness was not something my father was known for."

Vlad ran a finger along his wrist where the sleeve of his suit jacket stopped, remembering how it felt when his own father tied his hands together with wire, making him scrub the floors that way as punishment for interrupting a business dinner. Vlad was eight. The family dog had darted into the dining room and he was only trying to get him out.

Sometimes he could still feel the ghost of that wire. "Kindness was not my father's way either."

Her expression softened. "What happened to your family? What happened here all those years ago?"

His throat went tight. "Something terrible."

Balthazar squeaked softly, a gesture to show Vlad he was here for him. Guilt washed over the count for forgetting his dear friend was even in the room.

"Balthazar said you were on your way to Shademoss."

Excitement heightened her voice. "Yes, I'm moving there. I've grown tired of my village and want to see how the more civilized live." Emerald eyes sparkled as she spoke. "Endless possibilities await me in a place where I can actually *live* and not just bide my time washing clothes, working a field, or tending children."

He'd only begun to learn about her and Lenore was already fated to leave. A sharp pain started in his chest. Something like abandonment, though he didn't even know her.

"Do you have children?" Vlad asked tentatively.

"No. No husband and no children. Free to do as I please."

He tapped his fingers on his knee. Asking her if she wanted those things would be prying, so he changed the subject. "You must be famished. May I make you something to eat?"

Lenore pressed a hand to her stomach. "A meal would be nice."

"I shall retreat into the garden and be back after I tend to your mule. There is a well near the stables and I shall bring him some grass."

"I can water Marty while you're in the garden," she offered.

"It is far too cold out there for you, madam. Allow me," Vlad said, unable to contain a smile that showed his fangs.

Her cheeks flushed again. He wasn't sure what it meant.

"I'll be fine. I'm heartier than I look." The half-smile she gave him stopped his breathing.

When her smile faded, Vlad realized he'd been staring and quickly looked away. "I would be happy to take care of both tasks. Stay here and keep warm."

"I am capable of caring for my own animal. I want to see to Marty myself."

Vlad deflated. He'd done nothing to earn her trust, but he knew that's what kept her from accepting his offer. He bowed, a polite movement from his youth that came rushing back with surprising ease. "As you wish, madam. Balthazar, will you show Lenore where the well is?"

The bat nodded. "Yes, sire."

# VLAD AND FRIENDS

Vlad entered the foyer and opened the closet where he kept his winter garments. It was still snowing, so he donned his top hat, gloves, and cloak.

He heard Lenore and Balthazar talking, sounding a bit like arguing. He would have a talk with Zar tonight. His friend was never that prickly.

Vlad dug up potatoes in the garden under the light of the moon. He'd planted them a month earlier than was typical after noticing the merange trees kept their leaves curled longer than usual. He was thrilled finding the potatoes had grown to full size. As he worked, Vlad thought of all the tasks he needed to complete for Lenore.

Feed her. Clothe her. Ready a room for her. Retrieve the cart Zar mentioned had broken down on the road.

He put the potatoes in his cloak pockets, smiling like a giddy kid at the chance to get to spend time with another person. And such a beauty. He'd make her see him as a man, not a monster. Show her that his heart and words were pure. Make her see him as a friend.

And if he was lucky, perhaps something more.

# 6

## Lenore

Balthazar cut her off. "I will show you how to do it."

She pushed his furry body aside, grimacing at the strange feel of leathery wings brushing her hand. "I know how to use a well."

The bat mumbled some choice words far too austere for the refined way he presented himself.

She grabbed the long rope attached to a bucket and lowered it into the water.

Balthazar landed on the ring of stones making up the well. "You sure you don't want my assistance?"

"Your snarkiness is unnecessary, bat."

"So is your stubbornness, human."

An echo sounded as the bucket hit something hard.

Balthazar smirked.

Of course the water was frozen. No problem. She'd dealt with this before. Lenore searched for a hefty rock.

"What are you doing?" Balthazar asked.

"Looking for something to break the ice."

"You will not throw anything down there!" He spread his wings to block her.

She chuckled. "A two-foot wingspan won't stop me."

"Maybe your good sense will. If you have any."

She picked up a rock and tossed it in the air. "How is it that you're able to talk?"

"Why do you want to know?"

Lenore smirked. "So it'll help me figure out how to make you stop."

He glared. "Do not throw that rock. You will contaminate the water. That is not how we do things here."

Someone's inability to think her capable sent Lenore's temper flaring, even if it was the opinion of a snooty bat. "I've been fetching water for years. I know how to do this. Now, move."

Balthazar showed her his two tiny fangs.

"You would be much more menacing if you weren't so small."

"And you would be much more tolerable if you weren't so stupid."

Lenore prepared to hurl the rock in his direction but someone caught her wrist.

Vlad towered over her. She yanked her wrist out of his grip and quickly moved away from him.

"What is going on here?" the count asked.

The two began talking over one another.

Vlad lifted a hand. "One at a time."

They both began again.

Lenore pointed at the bat. "He won't stop talking down to me."

"Sire, she was going to throw a rock down the well. I was simply trying to show her the proper way we do things."

"By being condescending..." she grumbled.

Vlad's red eyes darted between them both. Wordlessly, he approached the well and reached inside. Water stirred below, though he hadn't touched the crank to raise the bucket.

"When the well is frozen, there is a pipe on this side that can siphon water into the bucket from under the ice."

Balthazar lifted his chin, all too proud.

Vlad hauled the full bucket over the edge and effortlessly carried it toward the stables. He slid the barn doors back and their faces collectively bunched as rusty metal ground against itself, making an awful screeching sound.

Lenore realized for the first time that she hadn't seen any livestock on the grounds. What did Vlad do for food? He couldn't possibly hunt every day. Surely he had stores somewhere.

Marty popped his head over the stall door and snorted his greeting.

Balthazar flew ahead, purposely smacking her hair with the tip of his wing.

She would have yanked him out of the air if she wasn't certain Vlad would kill her for it. His regal attire and gentlemanly attitude didn't fool her. He may dress like a member of high society, but a polite demeanor couldn't overshadow his past viciousness.

However, she needed food, shelter, and to keep her life, so Lenore would step lightly around him.

Vlad poured in the water and smiled so wide as he pet Marty that his fangs were on full display. "Beautiful animal."

The sight made her take a cautious step back. She didn't want to offend again, but he was a predator.

Vlad noticed her movement and his smile faded. "I plucked some grass and left it on the other side of the barn. I shall fetch it." He disappeared, leaving her alone with Balthazar. If Lenore wanted to keep her life, she would need to be on the good sides of both the count and his wilful little friend, so she swallowed her pride and said, "You were right about the well."

The bat gave a proud squeak.

Vlad returned with a sack full of grass and emptied it into Marty's stall. "This is dry from my greenhouse. I will gather more for him tomorrow, but I had to put a tarp over the garden to keep a section of ground clear. Snow will fall hard tonight."

"How do you know?" she asked.

A somber look crossed his face as he stroked Marty's neck. "The only positive to being an abomination of nature is the ability to understand it. To feel one with it."

Hearing the count refer to himself as an abomination wasn't what she expected. Self-loathing wasn't something monsters should be capable of, should they?

Moonlight shone on his smooth, pewter skin, perfectly void of facial hair, making the obscenely large man slightly boyish in his appearance. The slight turn of his head revealed a misty, pensive gaze.

He was hurting. Lenore wondered why.

Vlad walked away abruptly. "We should get back inside before you catch a chill. Marty will be safe and warm in here. I shall check on him in the morning."

Balthazar flew to the count and landed on his shoulder. The pair made their exit as she trailed after them, watching the way they interacted. Such an odd sight, yet there was no undercurrent of violence in either of their natures. At least from outside appearances.

Vlad held the door open for her, so she offered him a smile. He blushed, and the sight was so human. So ordinary. So...strange.

A barrage of swirling winds knocked Lenore about as soon as she stepped outside. Before she could put her hood on, hair came free of both braids and whipped her face, stinging her cheeks. Thank God she had somewhere warm to sleep tonight. Another night in the woods would have been perilous. She followed Vlad into the castle and removed her boots, setting them next to his and chuckling at the sight.

"What is it?" he asked, hanging up his hat.

"Your boots are massive compared to mine. You make me look like a kid."

He laughed. "Sometimes I forget how different my size is from most people." He began removing his cloak and pointed to a coat rack in the corner. "You may hang your coat there."

While Lenore fidgeted with a stubborn sleeve, a shadow grew taller on the wall in front of her. She whirled, finding Vlad standing dangerously close.

He froze. "I was going to help you with your coat."

"Sorry. You just...scared me." This close, the smell of loamy earth and balsam came barreling back. A scent she recognized as the same one from his chair in the Great Hall.

Balthazar must have flown off somewhere, as Lenore was alone with the hulk of a man taking up most of the space in the dark entryway. Shadows shrouded the master of the house in shades of gray and black, clinging to him like they were a living thing.

She swallowed hard.

Vlad seemed to sense her unease and stepped back.

Nervously smoothing her skirt, Lenore tried to make conversation. "Do you always dress so formal?"

He noted his attire. An immaculate black and white tuxedo with a vest and the collar buttoned up completely, finished with a white satin bowtie. A single strand of black hair fell out of place when he looked up, curling at the end over his forehead. He smoothed it back. "It's all I know."

Frozen in time and unable to evolve with a growing society.

There was a strange pinch in her heart. The enigma standing only a few feet from her didn't seem capable of the horrors of his past, amplifying Lenore's curiosity. *Why was he being so kind? Why hadn't he killed her yet? Was it all for delayed gratification?*

Maybe there was more to his story and people had been wrong about him.

Vlad watched her with intense curiosity, looking like he wanted to speak but didn't know what to say. His honed stare and the cold permeating the walls made Lenore shiver.

He shrugged out of his jacket and held it open for her. Against her better judgement, she gave him her back and slipped one arm in the giant sleeve.

When his fingertips gingerly brushed her neck as he folded the collar, Lenore gasped. The sound echoed in the empty space. Despite the warmth the jacket offered, her skin pebbled in goosebumps from his proximity and delicious scent.

A soft finger trailed down her neck over the goosebumps, making Lenore arch her neck. She'd never been touched so gently. So reverently.

Another noise came out of her. No, not her. A soft moan from the mouth breathing heat along her throat.

*Fangs.*

She whirled.

Vlad's arms were frozen around her, fangs nowhere in sight. "I..." he stuttered.

Lenore couldn't move. Didn't know if she wanted to. The count was handsome and he'd been nothing but a gentleman, but it was the care ensuring she was comfortable that muddled her feelings.

Crimson eyes searched hers. He touched a frizzy strand of hair surrounding her face. "Your hair is...nice. Gold. Like honey."

"Your hair is nice too," she said, feeling a bit foolish with the response. Lenore reached up to smooth back the curl that had popped free again dangling against his forehead.

A throat cleared.

Vlad moved away from her in that jarring speed of his, smacking into the banister with brutal force. "I uhh...I was just...She was cold."

Balthazar expressed his displeasure with a snort. "I found what you requested, sire."

"Thank you, Zar." Vlad righted his sleeves though there was nothing wrong with them and patted his vest. He smoothed back his hair, fixing the piece in front. The motion emphasized the muscles in his arm pressing against the perfectly white dress shirt.

Her stomach fluttered.

He gestured to the doorway that his companion blocked. "Lenore, will you accompany me to the kitchen? I shall make dinner."

She wrapped his jacket around her and hid a smirk, slipping past the churlish little bat. There was even less light in the kitchen and Lenore bumped into the edge of something solid. "Ow."

"Are you all right?" Vlad asked.

"I can't see anything in here."

A whoosh of air blew her hair back, and the room seemed to expand, like his presence had gone. A moment later, he appeared directly in front of her, red eyes the only thing she could see.

Lenore shrieked.

He jumped back. "I'm sorry! Did I frighten you?"

She pressed a hand to her forehead. "You can't keep doing that when I'm not ready. Your speed is alarming."

His eyes fell to his feet. "I'm sorry. I'll do better next time."

She hated the hurt in his voice. Like a boy being disciplined by his father. A father who'd apparently been as unkind to him as Lenore's father had been to her.

She gently gripped his arm. "I didn't mean it in a harsh way. I'm just not used to it. You just startled me, that's all."

He looked to where her hand rested, eyes wide like he'd seen a ghost.

Lenore quickly released him, unsure if she had crossed a boundary.

Balthazar scowled like she had.

Vlad opened his hand, revealing a box of matches. "I forgot you don't have nocturnal vision so I asked Balthazar to look for these."

He began rummaging through the cabinets in the spacious kitchen until he found a few candles. After placing candles around the room and lighting them, Vlad pulled out a chair by the counter. "For you, madam."

He was so well-mannered that it was difficult not to find him endearing. After pushing her chair in and setting the potatoes he'd dug up on the counter, he made for the door. "Zar, can I speak to you in the hall?" Vlad gripped the doorframe and smiled. "We'll be back in a moment."

Lenore settled into her seat, snuggling into the luxurious jacket she'd been given. She was in a royal's castle with a man about to make dinner for her. She could get used to this.

# 7

## Vlad

"I need you to go."

Balthazar reared his head back. "Sire?"

Vlad peeked into the kitchen and kept his voice low. "I want to speak with her alone. Without any interference."

Balthazar flinched like he'd been hit. "I don't understand. You want me to hide away?"

"Not hide, just find some way to occupy your time for a little while."

"You want me to sequester myself so you can flirt with that woman? Cast me aside like I haven't lived in this house for over a century?"

Vlad gave him a pointed look. "You two don't get along, which we need to discuss later. You need to be more welcoming."

"Welcoming! She—"

"Keep your voice down!"

Balthazar grumbled.

"I want to get to know her and you being here will impede that. Just for tonight. Please?"

There was a flash of hurt in Zar's eyes. "Fine," he gritted out.

Vlad would apologize later by bringing honeysuckles back from his nightly feeding—Zar's favorite. If he could find any. The early winter would kill most of them off, but some of the hardier plants still grew by the river where he hunted.

When he entered the kitchen, Lenore looked up from rolling a potato in between her hands. Her cheeks were still flushed from the cold, hair windblown.

She was so pretty. And cute. And nice. Vlad shook his head. He needed to calm down.

"So, what's for dinner?" Lenore asked. "Can I help?"

The nerves kicked in. He had no idea how to make a proper meal. "You are my guest. You relax, and I will take care of everything."

Her ashy brows knitted together. "I'm capable of helping."

He retrieved a pan from a cabinet and dropped it, the tin clattering obnoxiously loud. "No, no. It's okay. I'm sure you're capable, but it would be my honor."

Lenore still looked at him in that strange way. The way his mother used to before she scorned him. *Had he upset her?*

Vlad fetched a fresh pail of water from the basin and poured it into the pot. He grabbed a knife with a rusted handle and one of the potatoes. *How hard could it be to cut a potato?*

In his youth, he'd often run through the kitchen chasing the visiting noble's children, but he'd never stayed long enough to learn how to prepare a meal. Vlad guessed and cut the vegetable in half.

"You aren't going to peel them first?"

He chuckled awkwardly. "Right. How silly of me."

Lenore leaned back in her chair, shifting under his jacket. Some primal part of him came alive as he observed how she looked in his clothing. It swallowed her, but in a way that made him feel like he was protecting her. Even if it was only with a garment.

Vlad began peeling the potato. "I admit, I don't really have much for you except these and some berries."

"You don't have meat?"

He shook his head.

"What about flour? Salt? Sugar?"

His palms began to sweat. "I uhhh...I'm a bit low on everything."

Her nose wrinkled as she watched him peel the potatoes and he sensed he was doing it wrong.

"Wait a second. You said dinner for 'me'. If you don't have anything else here, what will *you* eat?"

His cutting hand froze. Vlad didn't meet her eyes. He knew the question would come at some point, but there was no way to prepare himself for how to answer. He didn't want to lie, but he didn't want to scare her.

"Vlad?"

His name on her lips shocked his system. So much so that Lenore's wary tone missed him completely. A human hadn't said his name since...Since when? When was the last person to use his given name? Vlad couldn't remember.

He set the knife down and rested both palms on the table, sighing. "You may notice I am a bit different than you."

She tilted her head. "Yes…"

*How was he going to tell her?* Surely she would bolt out the door from the truth, but he couldn't lie to those round, emerald eyes staring at him.

Vlad rubbed the back of his neck until he could finally hold her apprehensive gaze for longer than a few seconds. "I will tell you everything you want, Lenore. Whatever you ask. I just don't want you to be disturbed by the answers."

Her arms shifted under the bulk of his jacket. Was she going for a knife? Did she even have one on her? He'd been so transfixed by someone showing up on his doorstep he'd forgotten to check if she was armed.

He backed away. "Wait! I—"

Lenore removed her empty hands from the cloak and he felt like a fool.

"What's wrong?" she asked.

"I just thought you might be going for a knife. That's what the others have tried."

"How many 'others' have you prepared potatoes for?"

He laughed at the silly question. "You're the first person that's been in this castle since…everything."

Lenore nodded slowly. "There's a lot to you I don't know, but you've been polite and accommodating. You could have killed me when I first showed up, but you didn't.

He would never.

"So why don't we both share our truths. You tell me something about you and I'll tell you something about me." She snuffed out the tension by resting her elbows on the table and offering him a beautiful smile. "You first."

Vlad leaned against the counter, the potatoes forgotten. *Best to be straightforward and honest.* "I drink the blood of animals for food."

Her eyes blew wide. "Is that why you have Balthazar? To feed on?"

He burst out laughing. "No, no. He is a friend, not food. I kill large animals."

She blinked.

*Oh no.* He hadn't mean to say 'kill'. "I try to go for the old or sick ones. I don't savagely attack any animal I see, but I'm sure you know that already."

Her brows furrowed. "What do you mean? How would I know that?"

He looked at her quizzically. "I drain the animals I leave for the people of your town completely of blood. Surely you've seen them."

The crease in her forehead deepened. "You leave animals for us? Where?"

"Halfway down the mountain. The men retrieve them after I feed so the meat doesn't go to waste."

Lenore scoffed, smiling strangely. "That's what Balthazar meant by you had dealings with Newthorn. I knew something was off! Alvin and his friends are shit hunters." She shook her head. "Dirty little liars. They would return to the village boasting about their great kill. I should have known those puny men were incapable of providing for themselves."

While she continued bashing the men of her village, Vlad realized he needed to boil water. He added a pot to the stove and lit the fire.

"You truly didn't know?" he asked.

She played with the end of one of her braids. "They were good at faking it. How long have you been doing that?"

"Forty years or so. I had a deal with the elders that they could have the meat if they kept the townsfolk from trying to harm me and my home."

She stopped fiddling, eyes darting back and forth like she was calculating something. "That's why they were so insistent the 'monster on the mountain' was real. So we wouldn't go find out for ourselves."

Vlad flinched at the expression. "I didn't know people still called me that. I thought maybe if I gave them something they might view me differently. I had no idea they still feared me so."

Lenore shared a pained glance with him. "You seem incredibly nice. Not at all like what I've heard. I don't see you as a monster anymore."

His heart did somersaults. "You don't?"

"Well, aside from your eye color, skin tone, fangs, and enormous height, you're not so different from me." The dimples as she chuckled began thawing his cold heart. Warming him from the inside out. He'd never felt a stirring like it.

"I suppose I'm not like most men."

The light amusement in her doe eyes shifted into something else as she ran her gaze over him. "You are quite pleasant to look at. Not as scary as I thought you'd be."

Vlad wasn't sure he was breathing. Was she interested in him? No, it couldn't be.

Water hissed on the stove as bubbles poured over the rim in a fury. Panicking, he lifted the pot until the bubbles receded, then placed it back on the heat and dropped in the potatoes.

"Do you know what you're doing?" Lenore asked.

"Is it that obvious?"

The sound of her laughter dusted away the cobwebs in his heart. He could listen to it for hours. "Leave them in for about twelve minutes. They're ready when you can poke them with a fork and it goes through easy."

"I shall make a note of that."

As they waited on the potatoes, Lenore watched wax drip down the side of a candle. "If you only drink blood, why do you bother growing a garden?"

"I grow fruit for Balthazar in the greenhouse, but I also grow vegetables because it's something to do. A living thing I can nurture and care for." He wasn't sure if he liked how easy it was to be vulnerable with her, but it might be years before he spoke to another person again. The thought made him look out the window. Snow came down heavier, and he rejoiced on the inside.

"That's so sad," Lenore said.

"It's pathetic."

"No. Not pathetic at all. I can't imagine how difficult it must be to not have human contact. Have you truly been alone all this time?"

"You're the first guest I've had. I do have a delivery boy who comes when I send a pigeon for items I run out of. Thread, fabric, candles. Though I don't use candles often since Balthazar and I can see fairly easily in the dark."

She perked up. "Is that why your eyes are that color?"

He rubbed his wrist, discomfort heating his skin. "Part of the reason." Not wanting to explain further, Vlad changed the subject and began speaking excitedly. "I can send word to my delivery boy and request any food you want. He can be here in a couple days."

"I'll be leaving tomorrow so you don't have to go through the trouble."

He flicked his head to the window behind her. "Don't think you'll be able to if this keeps up."

She noted the violent snowstorm brewing and frowned.

*Did she want to leave already?*

"You can stay as long as you want. I had Balthazar pick out a room for you upstairs. You'll have your own washroom and there are plenty of clothes in the wardrobe you can wear." He hoped it would be enough to entice her.

"That's very generous of you. I'm sure I smell terrible from my travels. I've probably ruined your jacket."

"It looks good on you."

Her eyes flew to his and Vlad shirked his forwardness by searching for a fork. After poking the potatoes and watching them break apart as she'd said, he spooned them into a bowl, grabbed the berries he'd picked, and handed Lenore the fork.

Vlad stared at the bowl of pitiful beige offerings and sparse fruit as the inadequacy of the meal loomed over him. "I'm sorry I don't have spices or anything else to give you."

"That's okay. I have some dried meat in my pack I can eat tomorrow. Thank you for making me dinner."

"I will bring your pack to your room for you. I folded the blankets and kept everything together just as you had it."

Each smile Lenore gave him ignited his heart. Vlad watched her eat in the flickering candlelight in a state of awe. Every movement she made was something new and intriguing to decipher.

"You said you would share a truth me with, and I'm curious, what is it you hope to find in Shademoss?" he asked.

Her face lit up. "I've been thinking I want to start a flower shop, but I also have experience with animals, so perhaps working with them in some capacity. That's the thing, I can do anything I want! I finally have an opportunity to explore what it is that makes me happy."

The passion in her voice as she spoke made it difficult not to be enraptured by her every word. What he would give to be that excited about something.

"Well, I hope you get all it is that you want." Instead of continuing to stare at her as she ate, Vlad excused himself. "I shall go prepare your room and draw you a hot bath. If you finish before I'm through, you're welcome to wait in the Great Hall. I'm sure Zar will be wanton for company."

She wiped her mouth. "Thank you, Vlad."

The effect this woman had on him, making him stutter and blush with the simple use of his name. He scurried out of the kitchen before he could say something daft.

Vlad poked his head into the Great Hall. The fire was still going, but Balthazar wasn't in either of his usual spots. He would find the bat later. He climbed the wide black staircase to the second floor and entered the third room on the right. The one visiting duchesses used when his family hosted nobles from foreign countries.

Vlad entered the forgotten space, lit a few candles, and got to work.

# 8

## VLAD

The count admired his work. Satin red sheets covered the four-post bed layered with a thick duvet he'd found in the closet. Even having sat untouched, the bedding still smelled relatively fresh. He would try and find lavender in the morning to help scent the space.

The hearth raged, heating the room to a temperature far too warm for his cold-blooded nature, but he thought Lenore would like it. Vlad knelt by the claw foot tub and twisted the handle. The pipes groaned in their awakening. He prayed the plumbing running under the hearth still worked and that the water would heat properly from the fire.

Brown water sputtered into the tub, but after a few seconds, it ran clean. Another minute later, and the water came out warm.

Vlad rifled through the cabinets under the washbasin. He hadn't ventured into most of the rooms when he'd first returned, other than clearing the castle making sure no animals or people lied in wait. He found shavings of something smelling faintly of vanilla and an unused bar of soap.

After placing the items on top of a plush towel draped over the side of the copper tub, Vlad pulled some of the curtains back to let in the moonlight. Its reflection rippled across the water as the tub continued filling and steam began to rise.

Outside, fat flurries and a fresh blanket of snow whitened the night, providing a serene contrast to the warm wood furniture, the red-toned rugs, and the candles burning inside.

He hoped Lenore would find it adequate.

When the tub had finished filling, Vlad sprinkled in the vanilla shavings. He checked that none of the candles on the windowsill were in danger of being too close to the curtains before making his way out of the bedroom, smiling at what he'd created.

He wished more than ever he could see his reflection, blindly fussing with his hair and trying to make sure each strand lay flat to one side, but the ornery one in front flopped along his forehead. He and Balthazar used each other to check their appearances, and Vlad wondered if Zar had returned. He checked his friend's room on his way downstairs, frowning when it was empty.

In the Great Hall, Lenore lay curled up in his jacket, draped across the green velvet chaise. One arm dangled off the side and her face was smashed into the pillow, mouth open as she snored.

He chuckled. Had he really taken that long to prepare her room? Perhaps she was just exhausted. It had been a whirlwind of a day, full of more excitement than he ever could have hoped for.

Vlad carefully scooped her up and slowly made his way to her room. He couldn't stop focusing on the woman in his arms. Vlad relished in another's proximity and the warmth Lenore radiated. Knowing she'd felt safe enough to fall asleep around him was progress he hadn't expected. She had every right to be wary after learning her people still thought of him as monstrous and had continued to feed her that lie.

He would never hurt her, or anyone, for that matter. Vlad wished the humans had never seen him the first few days after he'd been turned into a vampire.

A child with crimson eyes and bloodstained teeth, half-crazed with bloodlust would be a frightening sight for anyone. They didn't understand that time in his life had been fleeting, so rumors of a cannibalistic, psychopathic child loose in the mountains became the story that grew with him as he aged.

He shouldered the bedroom door open and was about to lay Lenore on the bed when she woke with a start. She screamed, flailing so wildly he almost dropped her.

"It's okay! It's just me," Vlad said, setting her down.

She pressed a palm to her forehead, chest heaving. "Sorry. Forgot where I was for a second."

*Was he really so frightening?* He'd do anything to put her mind at ease, even changing parts of his appearance, if able.

She looked around the room. "You did all of this for me?"

He nodded and pointed at the tub, the steam fogging up half the window. "I found some bathing items for you and set them on the towel."

"Oh, God. I can't wait to sink into that water. My baths back home were lukewarm, at best." Lenore ran her fingers over the satin bedding as she perused the space. "This is beautiful fabric."

"Only the best for you."

She set her lovely eyes on him and handed over his jacket. "Thank you for letting me borrow it."

He bowed. "It's my pleasure. I shall leave you to it. And I won't bother you in the morning, so please sleep as long as you'd like."

As she began untying her braids, Vlad had the urge to run his fingers through her golden locks. Was her hair as soft as it looked?

"Thank you, Vlad. I appreciate all you've done for me and Marty. Thank you for taking us in."

His heart swelled. "You're very welcome, madam. Enjoy your night. There are day clothes and nightwear in this wardrobe."

"Are the homes in Shademoss decorated this lavishly?" she asked. "I can't wait to see it for myself. I've always wondered."

Her smile wrecked a part of him that stupidly hoped she wasn't excited to be leaving the castle. Asking Lenore to stay a while after only half a day of knowing her was an idiotic thing to do, but the request almost came out of his mouth.

Vlad swallowed the words before he could make a fool of himself. "I'm not sure. Sweet dreams, Lenore." When he closed the door behind him, Vlad shut his eyes and sighed. She wouldn't be able to leave just yet, thanks to the snowstorm, so he would relish in the time he did have with her. A smile slid across his face. "At least I'm not alone tonight."

"I see I've already been replaced." Balthazar sat on the banister, sulking.

"You know I didn't mean it like that, Zar."

"Then how did you mean it, sire?"

He pushed off the door. "Let's continue this conversation downstairs."

Balthazar huffed but he followed. Vlad had lit candles lining the hallway on his way to ready Lenore's room, surprised that the light didn't hurt his eyes. Sunlight could be harsh and stabbing, but the warm glow of a beeswax candle was softer than he remembered.

How much had he forgotten of his childhood?

When they entered the Great Hall, Vlad grabbed a pail of water and doused the fire.

"No nightly game?" Zar glanced at the chess set.

"Not tonight. I need to get some sleep to make sure I'm up early so I can make her breakfast."

"What about feeding?"

Vlad knew he needed to, but if Lenore needed him for any reason, he didn't want to be away from home. "I'll do it in the morning."

"Sire, you need to feed. And the humans need their offering."

The curtains were drawn and the cushions on the chaise rearranged to their proper place as Vlad tidied up. "I will take care of all of that in the morning. The people can go one day without me serving them."

Zar followed the count into his quarters, listing his complaints. "Why are you changing everything for her? She won't be here for long. You're letting that foul-mouthed farm girl disrupt your routine. You must feed, sire."

Vlad knew what this was really about. "I apologize for asking you to leave earlier. That was wrong of me. I was just anxious to converse with someone of my species." He made sure to look his friend in the eye to show he was genuine. "I hope you can understand."

Balthazar's tight mouth loosened. "I do not wish to be cast out again."

Vlad draped his jacket over one of the wingback chairs and removed his cuff links. Gold ones with embossed Dracula family crests that matched the one on the main gates. He'd taken refuge in his parent's old bedroom but promptly changed the decor and rearranged the furniture. "You won't be. You have my word."

"Good. It's bitter cold out there."

"Were you outside the whole time?"

"I was hunting, but I also just needed…space."

Tension filled the room. Unfamiliar and uncomfortable. Never before had they had been on cautionary terms. Spats were had here and there, but their friendship always prevailed.

Vlad placed the cufflinks in the box on his dresser. "I am glad to have you back, friend. I hope you can forgive me."

Balthazar cracked a toothy smile. "Couldn't get rid of me that easily, sire. Even for a pretty face."

Their mutual laughter eased the strain between them.

As Balthazar made for the door, he said, "I will do my best to befriend the girl. Not for her sake, but for yours."

Vlad tipped his head. He would take what he could get.

The bat flew into the room directly across the hall. Once a nursery, as he didn't require much space. A rope hung from the door handle Balthazar used to open and close the door, never fully shutting it.

No one could replace his furry friend who had kept Vlad from going insane and completely losing himself while in captivity. The friend who had agreed to stay once they were free and had been here for many years. Vlad owed everything to him.

"Zar."

The bat poked his head into the hall.

"You're the truest friend I've ever had. That will never change."

Balthazar grinned and bowed his head. "And you are mine, sire."

# 9

## BALTHAZAR

Nothing was worse than being at odds with his dearest friend. They'd parted on good terms the night prior, but that didn't stop Balthazar from nervously fidgeting with the collar around his neck as he readied for the morning.

Though merely a white strip of fabric joined by a single black button, it was his most prized possession. Hand-sewn by the count after he'd asked Balthazar to live in the castle with him. Two outcasts in their own respects who had nowhere else to go had made a home together, and for many years there was peace between them.

Until the girl interrupted.

He would make good on his promise to befriend her, though he knew the task ahead to be difficult. The count was mild-mannered and easy to get along with. Not stubborn, crass, and strong-willed like the farm girl. He wasn't sure what Vlad saw in her. Pretty on the outside but downright contrary in her demeanor. If she was to deserve his friend's attention, Balthazar would have to straighten her out.

Satisfied with the collar's position, he took the string tied to the door handle of his bedroom between his teeth and tugged until the gap was wide enough for him to slip through.

Normally, he would have gone downstairs and picked berries from the greenhouse for breakfast, if he hadn't gotten his fill of insects the night before. The cutout in his window Vlad made allowed the bat easy access to the outdoors and kept his room chilled. Just the way he liked it. Requiring blood to survive like the count, but not as much, Balthazar fed on insects and mice though he much preferred the sweet taste of fruit.

When he made it to the girl's room, he frowned at the slew of curse words coming from inside. Very improper language for a lady.

"Miss?" he called out.

The cursing stopped. "Yes?"

"May I come in?"

A deep sigh. "Sure." Lenore opened the door, clutching a sky-blue dress to her chest.

Upon entering, Balthazar did a quick scan for any weapons she may have accidentally left out, satisfied when nothing caught his eye. He would scour her room later to make sure. If her broken cart was a rouse and she was here to steal Vlad's money or try and harm him, Balthazar would find out.

Lenore stumbled over the floor length dress.

"You're going to crinkle the chiffon if you keep stepping on it," he said.

She yanked the dress further up her body. "I can't reach the strings. They go all the way up the back." Lenore reached behind her, grunting when the ties slipped out of her grip. "Damn things."

"Here. Let me help you."

"You're not going to bite me when my back's turned, are you?"

He showed his fangs. "I just might."

She glared at him.

"Just turn around." Balthazar took one of the ties in his mouth and flapped backwards in large swoops, pulling it taut.

"Hold your finger here," he said with a mouthful of satin, pressing his nose to where he was referencing.

They worked together tightening the ribbons down the length of the bodice. Lenore blindly tied the remaining strings in a bow and turned around, smoothing the front of a garment far too dignified for someone of her caliber.

"How did women in this era ever put these on by themselves?"

"They didn't. They had hand maids to assist them. Did you put the corset on that goes underneath?"

She pointed at the item in question lying on the bed. "You mean that body prison? Absolutely not."

Balthazar shook his head. "If you're going to dress like a proper lady, you should wear the options provided."

"You wrap that thing around yourself and then tell me you want to wear it all day."

They held a defiant staring contest until Lenore eventually looked away, choosing to admire herself in the mirror instead. "This is beautiful fabric though. I'm almost afraid to wear it. Don't want to ruin something so clearly expensive."

At her mention of money, Balthazar perked up. "If you're here to steal the count's fortune, you'll have quite a difficult time locating it in a castle this large."

A hand went to her bosom like she was offended. "I am not a thief. I'm here because my cart broke."

It was hard to tell by her round eyes and cheeks that made her appear soft and feminine if she was a lying serpent of a woman or telling the truth. But he'd promised to befriend her, so for Vlad's sake, Balthazar swallowed his barbed response. "Apologies, miss. We got off on the wrong foot. I'm only looking to protect my friend. You wouldn't be the first person to try something under false pretenses."

She began pinning half of her hair up. "Vlad mentioned that last night. How many people have done that? Was he threatening with the others who came here?"

Zar was quick to the defense. "He is the kindest person I have ever known. Even after everything that witch did to him. He's never tried to harm anyone who's come here with intent to do the same."

Her voice came out soft. "A witch made him the way he is?"

Revealing Vlad's past on his behalf might not be the best idea, but the girl needed to know who the count was at his core.

"Those days are painful to recall. You'd think after one-hundred-and-forty years it'd get easier."

Days of watching his friend struggle in a cage made of the bones of the witch's failed experiments were nearly unbearable to witness.

# VLAD AND FRIENDS

Stuck in a small space with no way to avoid her tools, Vlad never stood a chance.

Lenore sat on the edge of the bed, looking at him expectantly.

"The witch did many experiments on the count before I came along. Poked and prodded him. Made him consume heaps of horrible concoctions she'd created. I was an accident. Flew into the wrong home at the wrong time. She turned me into this almost instantly, but with Vlad…"

Balthazar's eyes went misty. "She took her time with him. It's a miracle he's not a monster. She did everything to try and make him one."

"That's awful. Poor Vlad. And poor you. The folklore speaks of witches, but I never knew they actually existed." She wrung her hands together, sharing a pained glance with him. "I'm sorry for being so cross with you yesterday. I think we were both a bit on edge, but you and Vlad have shown me kindness. I apologize I haven't done the same."

Perhaps he'd been too quick to judge. The unfriendly blockade between them started to come down, and with it, a sincere admission. "With your arrival, I have seen the count more full of life than all the years I've known him. Please don't do anything to hurt him while you're here. He doesn't deserve any more pain."

"I don't plan to."

"Good." When she finished pinning up her hair, Balthazar made for the door. "Well, let's get you to the kitchen. Hopefully he has something for you other than those pitiful potatoes you were served for dinner."

She chuckled. "They weren't that bad."

"Has Newthorn robbed you of proper tastebuds?"

Lenore gathered her dress, walking awkwardly down each stair. "I've never had anyone volunteer to do anything for me. Those potatoes were the first meal I've had that I didn't have to make myself."

"Truly?"

"Truly."

It was possible the girl needed Vlad as much as he needed her. Two parts to work together as a whole. Zar didn't want to get ahead himself. The count's rapid infatuation was something he would need to keep an eye on, lest he make a crucial mistake.

"Why do you refer to him as the count?" Lenore asked. "He's sequestered himself here, so how can he hold a noble title?"

"The Malachian king took over these lands after the Dracula family's reign ended, so the title isn't a functionary one. Vlad was a young prince in his time, and he would have been considered a count in adulthood. I call him that to remind him of who he is and was, despite what happened.

Lenore was quiet for a moment. Reflective. "He's lucky to have you."

The bat's tiny heart beat with pride. "I'm sure he'll be just as eager to make this meal for you, but maybe after you eat we work on how to walk in a dress. What you're doing now is ghastly."

"What would you know about a dress?"

Balthazar arched his neck, showing off his collar. "I am a paragon of fashion. I know more than you think."

She rolled her eyes, grinning. "A talking bat who's full of himself. Typical man."

The sound of a bowl crashing to the floor rang out as they rounded the corner. Balthazar stifled a laugh at the chaos ensuing in the kitchen.

Vlad had every pot and pan on the counter with more utensils scattered about than could possibly be needed to prepare breakfast for one person. The bulky man looked ridiculous in a frilly pink apron clearly meant for someone half his size.

Zar was about to rib him for it when he caught sight of Lenore lingering in the doorway. Her cheeks turned pink as she chuckled behind the cover of her hand, but it was the way she looked at the count that made Balthazar hold his tongue.

Perhaps one day she would offer him more than friendship. He knew Vlad wanted her to stay and that he desperately needed human companionship, as Zar often craved companionship of his own species. Maybe he could try to mingle with the other bats soon. Hopefully his second attempt would go better than the first.

Vlad finally noticed them watching. Sweat glistened on his forehead as he labored over the stove. "I didn't think you'd be up so soon," he said to Lenore.

She hadn't stopped giggling. "Can I please help this time?"

He looked at the spatula in his hand like it was a foreign object, which it was. "Oh. Umm..."

Balthazar had never seen his friend so out of sorts. It was quite entertaining. He flitted over to the opposite side of the kitchen. "If

I may, sire, the girl might be able to keep you from burning her breakfast black."

Vlad didn't react. He was too busy letting his eyes linger on the swoop in the girl's neckline showcasing her ample cleavage.

Balthazar cleared his throat. He would have to teach the count the art of subtlety.

"I would love your help," Vlad said, snapping out of it. "I gathered a few pigeon eggs and some berries." He glanced at Balthazar.

The food in the greenhouse was for him, but Zar said, "I guess she can have some."

"Learning to share, are we?" Lenore teased.

He stuck up his nose. "Careful, or I'll take it all back."

If this was to be their relationship—verbal sparring and a battle for Vlad's attention—he would gladly take the girl on in a friendly game to see who would emerge the victor. Though, if it was all a trick, Balthazar would be the first to catch on and keep her from hurting either of them. He may be little, but he would protect his friend until his last breath.

"I sent a message to my delivery boy. I wasn't sure what kind of foods you liked, so I took a guess."

Lenore cracked the eggs over a pan, smiling at Vlad. Zar knew his friend well enough to know he was absolutely smitten with her by the goofy grin on his face.

Balthazar glanced out the window at the mention of the delivery boy. The snow was at least two feet deep. "How is he going to get here? The road will not be clear."

"I cleared part of it overnight. Pending no more snowfall, he could make it here in three days."

Zar looked closer and registered the tiredness in his friend's eyes. If he'd cleared the road, gathered breakfast, and fed, he must not have slept at all.

Vlad watched intently as Lenore walked him through a few helpful steps—temperature, cook time depending on the type of food, and recommended spices to pair with different dishes.

Once she'd finished eating and Balthazar had snatched a few raspberries off her plate, Vlad offered to give her a tour of the castle before setting out to retrieve her broken cart. He asked if Balthazar would like to join them on the tour, but he politely declined, choosing to give the count what he desired—alone time with Lenore. Besides, post-breakfast was when he went out for his hourly exercise flight.

As he watched Vlad lead the girl up the stairs, an unfamiliar emotion twinged his chest. Balthazar would need to learn how to share his friend with another, and selfishly, he wasn't sure if he was ready. What if she took up all his time? What if Vlad decided he preferred Lenore over him?

No, no, he would never do that.

He knew his friend's heart, but that didn't stop the worry from creeping in. Balthazar gazed out the window and let the falling snow entrance him until the pang of jealousy subsided and only happiness for his friend remained.

# 10

## LENORE

Vlad walked with his hands behind his back, pointing to paintings and explaining what each of the large rooms were used for in their heyday.

She marveled at the fine art and how nearly all the furniture was gilded. The variety of gorgeous fabrics in each room was staggering and the artifacts collected over time had such rich history she was happy to listen to as he spoke. Bedrooms lined the third and fourth floors, with drawing rooms and smaller ballrooms on the second floor.

"What's this room?" Lenore ventured inside before he had a chance to answer. The smell of polish, leather, and wood enveloped her senses. More settees, chaises, and candelabras, but they paled in comparison to the two instruments sitting in the corner.

"This is the music room." Vlad's posture straightened as he pointed to the biggest instrument she had never seen. "That is a grand piano. My grandfather's. This..." He picked up an odd looking instrument by the neck similar to a fiddle, but much, much larger. "Is a cello."

The shine on the amber instrument was extraordinary, and the piece certainly looked well loved. "Is this your favorite one to play? she asked.

He nodded.

Lenore plopped down on the settee in a less elegant way than she'd intended. She tried to adjust her legs the way a proper lady might sit in a dress like the one she wore but wasn't quite sure how. It all felt awkward and new, but she tried. "Will you play for me?"

Vlad's face lit up. He settled into a chair, grabbed the bow, and set the instrument that was nearly as tall as him in between his legs. He brought the bow to the strings and flashed his red eyes at her, grinning.

How quickly those eyes had turned from utterly terrifying to intriguing. Lenore knew what she was doing was unsafe. That letting her guard down around someone only partly human was folly, but he acted so *normal*. Damn her if she wasn't compelled to discover more about him.

"This is my favorite piece." The silver smile slid from his face, replaced with intense concentration. Vlad went somewhere else. Somewhere different than their reality as his eyes went distant.

Focused. Steady. Poised.

Lenore leaned forward in her seat, anxious to see what would happen next.

Vlad was a marvel.

The way he swayed with the music. The tones he could create that wrenched absolute heartbreak out of her. The kind of pain and hurt Lenore thought she knew.

A lackluster father. A dead mother. A stagnant life. None of it compared to the agony in his music.

Devastating beautifully in its melody, Lenore could do nothing but cry. Vlad lost himself in the song. With eyes closed, his face would twitch and relax, following the wave of the crescendo. He was able to shift her mood and stir things deep inside her chest Lenore wasn't ready to confront.

By the time he'd finished, she was sobbing.

He looked at her like he'd forgotten she was in the room. "You didn't like it?"

An absurd laugh came out of her. "Like it?" Lenore wiped the snot running down her nose, trying to hide it with her sleeve. "That was so unbelievably beautiful. I loved it."

His face contorted. "Then why are you crying?"

"Because it was so sad. I didn't know music could do this to me." She chuckled. "Look at me. I'm a mess."

Vlad rose and pulled a handkerchief from his breast pocket, handing it to her. "I didn't mean to make you sad. I thought—"

"No, no. It wasn't that. Your playing was phenomenal. There was just so much pain in it."

He sat next to her, rigid as stone like her crying made him uncomfortable. Lenore wasn't afraid of his proximity. She wanted to hug him. Wanted to know what happened that caused him such hurt.

"I find peace in it," he said, face drawn. "I didn't realize how it might sound to others."

Lenore finished blowing her nose and tried to hand the handkerchief back to him, but he lifted a hand. "Keep it."

She was about to ask him to tell her about the witch Balthazar mentioned when Vlad abruptly rose and offered her his hand. "We should be on our way. I still need to retrieve your cart while the snow has stopped."

His skin was cool to the touch. Large but gentle fingers curved around hers as he helped her rise.

Lenore stared up at him, dressed in a pristine suit with swept back hair, musical prowess, money, and a noble title that were all far above a poor farm hand from the valley. They must look like laughable opposites standing together.

Her shoulders slumped. He may be a creation of some deranged woman's schemes, but Lenore was the odd one out. How could she ever compare to someone like Vlad Dracula?

His brows scrunched as he looked her over. "Are you all right?"

"I'm fine." She quickly made for the exit, but there was no outrunning her embarrassment. They couldn't be more different, and the knowledge of her inadequacy chewed at her self-worth like a hungry wolf.

## VLAD AND FRIENDS

She let him show her the last area on the fourth floor with more hallways, paintings, and guest bedrooms, but when they passed his father's study, Vlad drew into himself. His words became few and far between and the gestures stopped altogether. A sensitive subject, so she didn't press.

Once they were in the foyer, the two readied themselves for the journey. The hefty wolf's fur coat of white and gray made the count appear even larger than he already was, dwarfing her as she slipped on her measly wool coat.

"Are you sure you want to go with me?" he asked. "The snow has stopped but the temperature has dropped significantly."

The wind howled, creaking the massive doors. Lenore didn't feel like trekking in the cold for a half hour, but he had done everything for her so far, so she wouldn't sit by and let him go alone.

"I'd like to go with you. Plus, I need to check on Marty."

"I fed and watered him a few hours ago, but if you'd like to see him for yourself, we can check on him."

She wasn't sure if it was hurt that sent his eyes to the floor, like he didn't think she trusted him, or if it was something else. Lenore gripped his arm in reassurance. "I just don't want that old mule to think I've forgotten him."

He gave her a tight smile. "Well then, we shall tend to him, but you will need more than what you're wearing."

The wool wasn't the warmest, but it would do. "My coat will hold up just fine."

Vlad opened a closet and pulled out a beautiful, sleek mink coat of the darkest black and a furry round hat of the same. "These were my mother's. You're welcome to them."

She ran her fingers through the mink. It was even softer than it looked. "I'm touched, but I can't wear your mother's clothes."

He frowned. "Why not? They aren't getting any use, and you'll need something heavier to withstand it out there."

Her headstrong nature rushed to the surface. "I've managed to survive for twenty-six years without it. I'll be fine."

"You are my guest. It is my job to take care of you and provide things I know will help. Newthorn is protected from the winds. You do not know how brutal they can be on the mountain."

His offer was kind, but listening to someone say they knew what was best for her was something Lenore had escaped in Newthorn. She didn't want to go back to it now. "I can manage."

"Lenore."

She opened the door and was hit with an arctic blast. Hair lashed her face and the cold bit at her skin.

Vlad pulled her back inside. "See?"

Flurries already collected on her lashes. "It's not that bad."

He unfolded the fur coat and opened it up for her.

Reluctantly, she slid her arms inside and stroked the furry sleeves. "I'm not used to luxuries like these."

Vlad handed her a pair of fleece-lined, leather gloves. No item of clothing she owned was half as soft and pliable. Lenore was afraid to put them on and ruin them.

"All you need now is this." Vlad went to put the mink hat on her head and paused. Ever so gently, he brushed her hair back. For such a strong man, his touch was tender. Like she was a mirror that might crack under the slightest pressure.

Instead of looking at what his fingers were doing, Vlad kept his eyes on hers. They stood as close as they had in the music room, but the touch of their fingers was different than the feel of him brushing his knuckles down her temple.

Her heart fluttered. The ethereal, silver of his skin and faintly purple-hued lips called to her curiosity. *Were his lips cold? Was he cold?*

Before she realized what she was doing, Lenore pressed two fingers to his supple mouth. "Warm," she whispered in surprise.

His lips parted. Vlad didn't make any attempt to move, and she couldn't decipher the look in his crimson eyes. Interest? Caution? What was it? Only when her neck began aching from looking up at him did Lenore realize she had drifted into his chest.

Deflecting, she snatched the hat out of his hand and put it on. That hot flash of embarrassment came barreling back. What would a wealthy, well-mannered man ever want with her?

Vlad cleared his throat and grabbed his top hat. "We best get going."

Balthazar was still out on his flight, so the two of them left the castle and set out into the mid-morning grey. The sun shone fiercely but the feathered clouds blurred the light, confusing the time of day.

Lenore walked close to Vlad, using him as a shield from the frenetic winds. He was right. She would have frozen if not for the coat he'd loaned her.

They checked on Marty, perfectly content and half asleep in his stall.

By the time they made it to the main road beyond the gates, the wind had died down enough that they could carry on a conversation.

Lenore was used to trekking across fields, but the mountain walk covered a much larger distance over ever-changing terrain. Lenore tried to hide her struggle as they traversed the deep snow. "Can I ask you something?"

"Anything."

"Balthazar told me a witch was the one that turned you into…" She didn't want to say 'monster', but she wasn't sure what to call him.

"A vampire."

She mouthed it silently. "What is a vampire, exactly?"

Vlad ducked under a branch dangling over the road. "The witch had many descriptions for me. None of which I cared for. Degrading, despicable names," he spat.

Knowing it was a delicate subject, she let him reveal parts of himself at his own pace.

"A vampire is what I am. I have not been able to find records of any others that have existed over time in my library, so I believe I am simply a product of her twisted machinations. A creature of the night who needs blood to survive. Someone who cannot see their own reflection and whose eyes are sensitive to light. A person no longer completely human. Someone with one foot in this world and another in the next."

"You can't see your reflection?"

He shook his head.

Lenore blinked furiously, trying to fathom how the witch could have done that. "What do you mean you have one foot in this world and another in the next?"

"I am essentially half-dead. My heart beats at half the speed it used to, my body temperature is halved, and..." he swallowed hard. "I age differently, and at a rate that seems to have slowed even more these past ten years."

"Does it feel different? Aging on a different timeline from others, I mean."

He shrugged. "I still feel like a man in my late twenties, though I am far older. My body feels youthful. I am strong and don't have aches and pains, and from what I can feel of my face, I believe I still look similar to how I did when I was turned."

She glanced at him out of the corner of her eye. "It is a handsome face, if you don't mind me saying."

He grinned awkwardly. Vlad didn't respond, but he walked closer to her, enough that their coats brushed as they crested the hill and the lump of her broken cart appeared ahead, nearly buried in snow.

"I wonder sometimes if what the witch told me was true," he said softly. The low tilt of his hat hid his eyes. "She wanted to make me immortal. I don't know if she succeeded."

Lenore stopped walking. "That's possible? How? Why?" A swirl of questions circulated in her head as she stood there like a gaping fish. "Is there anyone who can help you find the answers? A good witch, perhaps?"

He gave her a broken smile. "Everyone is afraid of the 'monster on the mountain', as you reminded me. I don't think anyone would be willing to help. I've never conversed with someone calmly until you." Vlad cupped her gloved hands with his. "You're the first person who's ever given me a chance to show I'm not like what people think."

The overwhelming urge to hug him flooded her good senses. So she did.

Vlad was a statue against her. Lenore wondered if anyone had ever hugged him. All those years alone in that big, dark castle with only Balthazar for companionship. Agonizing over the knowledge his parents gave him away. Had he ever been given affection? Ever known real love?

She hugged him tighter.

Vlad recovered from his frozen state and wrapped his arms around her, surrounding Lenore in warmth despite his lower body temperature. He buried his face in her hair, clinging to her in such desperation that a piece of her heart broke for him. She could feel the gratefulness for the years of solitude being eased in the simple gesture of a hug.

One hand cupped the back of her head, mouth shifting to her crown. "Thank you," he said in a broken whisper.

A branch snapped.

One moment she was shrouded in the safety of his arms, the next she was looking up at the sky. Lenore sat up, trying to make out what she was seeing.

Multiple black shapes muddled together up the road, but it was the sounds that gave it away first. Snarls and barks echoed as wolves pounced on Vlad. Sharp, white teeth flashed—vampire and wolf alike. His cloak was torn this way and that by violent, thrashing jaws until the fabric ripped in half.

"Vlad!" Lenore looked around for anything she could use to help.

Another wolf tackled him to the ground. The remaining three stalked him as if she posed no threat at all.

Vlad snapped the neck of the animal clawing its way up his body, clothing was in tatters, face scratched and bloody.

She stumbled through the snow, digging until the wet soaked through her gloves and she found a rock the size of her fist. She launched the rock at one of the two remaining wolves and hit its shoulder.

The wolf yelped, lips pulling back from its teeth as it stalked toward her.

Lenore kept the animal's slow pace as she backed away, luring it away from Vlad. Just a few more steps and she could use the cart for cover.

Vlad threw a dead wolf off him and tried to stand but he fell to the ground with a groan. "Hey!" he yelled as a distraction. "Over here!"

Two more steps.

The wolf lunged.

Lenore screamed.

Vlad tackled the beast and they crashed into the cart with such force that something cracked. Wood or bone, she couldn't be sure.

Lenore yelled his name, concern sucking all the air from her lungs.

He roared as teeth bit into his shoulder and tore his shirt. Blood spurted from his neck, but Vlad got a solid grip on the wolf and yanked it off him with an agonized yell. He slammed it into a tree until it was dead before tossing the beast into the pile of its fallen companions.

The forest went silent, save for Vlad's labored breathing as he struggled to stand. She made it to him just before his leg gave out.

Lenore caught him around the waist, struggling to bear his weight. She slung his arm around her shoulders and gripped his wrist tight.

Each of his ragged breaths must have been anguish.

"Can you walk?" she asked.

His face bunched. "I think so." Vlad took one step and his knee buckled.

Lenore would have crumpled had she not acquired the physical strength that growing up on a farm required. She was never more grateful for her upbringing than at that moment.

They began the trek back at a painstaking pace, and when the castle came into view, Vlad said, "I can make it the rest of the way on my own."

"Not a chance. I'm not letting go of you." Her thighs burned, but she wasn't about to let him go at it alone.

"I can do it."

Lenore chuckled, though she was severely out of breath. "You're as stubborn as me."

A small laugh came out of him. He tried to hide his grimace but was failing miserably. "I think you still have me beat."

They passed through the iron gates with the oversized family crest. Once foreboding, now a sanctuary.

He tried to free his arm from her grip but Lenore held fast. "You're not doing this on your own, Vlad. We're getting to the castle together whether you like it or not."

Just a few more steps until they were inside and she could assess his injuries. When they made it through the front doors, Vlad collapsed.

## 11

## LENORE

"What in God's name happened?" Balthazar flapped furiously.

Vlad groaned as she tried to sit him up, but he was practically dead weight. She gripped his face. "Vlad, can you hear me?"

His eyes rolled in the back of his head.

"Why are his clothes torn? Why is he bleeding? What happened?"

Lenore lightly smacked him on the cheek. No response. She placed a finger under his nose. The faintest puff of air came from his nostrils.

"Will you tell me—"

"Wolves," she snapped. "He needs to warm up. His skin is ice. Is the fire in the Great Hall still going?"

Balthazar stared at his friend.

Lenore waved a hand in front of his face. "Is the fire still going?"

"Yes, yes. I will set something up." Balthazar darted away.

As Vlad lay on the floor, she carefully peeled the remainder of his coat off, struggling to move his sluggish limbs. Amazingly, the cuts weren't bleeding anymore, though the gaping wound near his shoulder should have been spilling blood.

She thought back to what he said on their walk. About everything about him being halved. If he had half as much blood as a typical human, had he already lost most of it? The natural pale hue of his skin didn't help matters. Lenore couldn't tell his condition and that sent her into a panic.

"Zar! Hurry!" She smacked his cheek harder this time and Vlad jolted awake. "I need you to get up."

His eyes were dazed, head lolling to the side. With great difficulty, Lenore got him into a sitting position.

"We have to get you standing," she grunted.

Seeming in and out of consciousness, Vlad somehow managed to get on two feet. They stumbled into the Great Hall just as Balthazar flung the final pillow into a pile of others.

"Lay him here," Zar said.

Vlad practically fell into the plush palette, thankfully on his back.

"Why isn't he bleeding? He's cut everywhere," she said, feverishly looking him over.

"I...I don't know. I've only seen him hurt once since the witch, but never this bad." Balthazar's voice squeaked on the last word. His eyes watered as he sat on the edge of the pillow next to Vlad's head. "He was gorged by an elk while learning how to hunt, but he stitched himself up. I've never seen him like this. He's not—he's not dead. He can't be dead."

"Hey," Lenore said in a gentle but firm tone. "Look at his chest. He's still breathing. He'll be all right." She didn't know if he would, but she needed Zar to have a clear head.

She added more logs to the fire. "I need you to tell me everything you know about vampires. Has something like this ever happened to you?"

"I've only had minor scraps. Nothing this severe. I don't know much, just that the witch kept using that word. Vampire. Vlad stopped her from turning me into solely relying on blood, so I've never felt what it's like to lose a lot of it, or the overwhelming desire to consume it."

Lenore wished she had more to go on, but there was one thing she could do. "Make sure he doesn't stop breathing. I'm going to get warm water and towels to wash his wounds and patch him up."

"There is a medical box in the pantry but I don't know what's in it."

She returned minutes later with the aforementioned box and a few other helpful supplies, kneeling by his head. Vlad's lips had turned a deeper purple. She didn't know how long he had.

"Does he need water? Blood? What do I do?"

"He hasn't fed in a day and a half." Balthazar sighed. "I told him to go feed but he insisted on doing it later. I figured he would have fed while he was out clearing the road, but I know he wanted to get back here as soon as possible in case you needed him."

Her heart felt lodged in her throat. "He shouldn't have neglected his health because of me." She dabbed Vlad's shoulder with a warm, wet cloth, wiping away the blood that had dried around the gash.

"You've given him something to care for. Something other than me. It's not surprising he would forfeit his own health for the sake of someone else." Balthazar deflated as he watched his friend take shallow breaths. "It wouldn't be the first time."

Lenore moved to another wound higher on Vlad's neck, taking in his beautifully sculpted face. "He saved me," she said softly. "He kept the pack of wolves from getting to me using his body to shield mine. I'm guessing he's done something like that for you, too?" She rang out the bloody rag over the bucket and grabbed a new one.

Balthazar swallowed hard. "The night we decided to make our escape we made a pact. That if it was too dangerous, and only one of us was able to flee, to not come back for the other. Because the risk of getting captured again would mean a punishment worse than death for both of us."

Balthazar plucked a salve out of the box and set it next to her. "We both thought we'd make it out of that nightmare, but when part of the witch's house collapsed after Vlad set it ablaze, I got caught under the rubble. I yelled for him to go. To leave me. As we'd planned."

Her heart wrenched. How selfless and how loyal of a friend Vlad was. Their bond went beyond species and transcended into a beautiful friendship Lenore would count herself lucky to have.

"But he didn't leave you behind, did he?" she asked.

Balthazar smiled weakly. "No. No he didn't. He came back at great risk to himself. Nearly got caught again the process. The fool..."

Using a pair of scissors, she cut away the remainder of Vlad's vest and white dress shirt now stained maroon. Dark purple bruises blotted the left side of his ribs, but thankfully, there were only a few scratches. Once the salve had been dabbed onto the scratches, Lenore spread it on the deeper wound in his shoulder. "He sounds more like a good friend than a fool."

"He's the greatest friend I have ever known."

They shared a look, one that said if anything were to happen to Vlad and Balthazar lost him, he'd be losing a part of himself.

"I've never known a friendship like the one you two share," Lenore admitted. "There was a woman back home, Nina. She was kind and we were friendly toward one another, but I was so busy tending to the farm most days that I didn't bother trying to build a real friendship. It wasn't that I didn't want one, I just couldn't understand why no one in Newthorn ever wanted to leave. Ever wanted more. Nina was content to live in a mud-soaked village with her shit husband and I never understood why she wanted to stay."

Balthazar plucked out gauze from the kit, anticipating her next move. He laid the strips out neatly beside her. "Was there truly no one else who wanted what you do?"

"There may have been, but I kind of kept to myself. It's partly my fault, but I didn't have much time for socializing. In a farming village, the work never ends, and my father was useless at home. I had to do everything. It's why I have to go to Shademoss. I want to truly experience life, not just pass the years wondering what might have been."

There wasn't any blood on Vlad's lower half, but his leg had given out a few times on the walk back, so she rolled up his pants and found a giant bite wound on his calf.

Balthazar came closer to inspect. "God...I'm glad you're here. I never would have been able to tend to him myself if something like this happened with just the two of us."

Though it was her fault the count was injured, maybe she was destined to be here. To save him. Lenore shook her head. No, she didn't believe in fate. Problem solving was how one went through life, not relying on some magic in the stars.

"I'm glad I'm here too because he's going to need stitches." She fished around the kit and found a needle and thread.

Balthazar watched closely as she began sewing his friend's skin back together. "How did you learn to do these things if your father never helped? Did your mother show you?"

She smiled fondly. "I was thirteen when a fever took her, but she showed me how to do the basics. Cooking, sewing, washing. I taught myself everything else."

"A self-sufficient woman. That explains why you didn't want either of our help with anything when you first got here."

"Self-reliance is a necessity in life. You have to look out for yourself because no one else will."

Zar squeaked. He hopped back onto the pillow cradling Vlad's head. "You have both of us now. You don't have to do it all."

Her brows furrowed. "What do you mean I 'have' you?"

"I mean you don't have to leave until you truly want to. I know you want to go to Shademoss, but perhaps consider staying here a while longer. You'd be welcome."

She pulled the thread tight, closing up the gash. Lenore found herself wanting to know Vlad more, but how long could she stay in an environment not conducive to human life? She needed food, work, people.

"I'll consider it. First thing's first, we need to get him better."

Zar nodded. "Of course. His lips are a better color, but he needs blood. Lots of it. He had to drink a few small animals after the elk attack before he said he felt normal again."

"Can you get it while I finish up here?"

Zar frowned. "We don't keep blood on reserve."

"You don't have jars for emergencies?"

He scoffed. "This is not a macabre residence, miss."

She chuckled. "Sometimes I forget I'm talking to a bat who wears a dress collar. Jars of blood must be far beneath a man of your class."

He glared. "Now is not the time to make such jokes."

"Preparedness isn't a joke. You both need blood to survive. It makes sense to keep some on hand."

Zar's mouth tightened.

"You know I'm right."

He lifted his snout. "I am not used to being proved wrong. I don't like it."

Lenore discarded the bloody rags and used the back of her hand to feel along Vlad's arms, neck, and forehead. He was warming up.

Good.

She covered him with blankets to speed up the process.

Vlad's eyes moved behind his lids like he was dreaming. Gently, she brushed his temple with her knuckles. "Vlad, if you can hear me, Balthazar and I are going to hunt so we can get blood for you."

"I'm not leaving him."

"I don't know this area and I need you to help me navigate it before we lose daylight."

They both glanced out the window. The snow and wind had ceased, but they only had a couple hours before nightfall.

Balthazar sighed. "Fine. But we should leave a note in case he wakes while we're gone."

"Good idea."

"I'll get a pen." He flew off, and she went back to lightly tracing Vlad's cheek.

"You saved me, so don't you dare die on me, Vlad Dracula." She choked back a cry. "I still have to scold you for being so gallant."

His eyes continued their movement behind his lids, and she found herself desperately wanting to see their crimson color she'd once feared.

"Come back," Lenore whispered.

Balthazar returned and dropped a fountain pen in her hand. "There's parchment and ink over here."

After crafting a quick note telling Vlad where they were going, Lenore headed outside in her borrowed fur coat and hat with Balthazar flying beside her. She retrieved Marty from the stables and put on his bridle, telling herself Vlad would wake.

He had to. She wasn't worth dying for.

# 12

## Balthazar

Lenore rode into the woods with Balthazar clinging to her shoulder.

"Is it always this bumpy of a ride?" he asked. "I'm being tossed about like a carriage on cobblestones."

Marty snorted, spewing snot onto the snow.

*Very unsightly.*

"You can fly if you want." She steered her mount around a fallen log with one hand, holding a bow in the other. The mule struggled to find his footing, and with only a saddle pad they found in the tack room and no saddle, Balthazar was uncertain they wouldn't slide off his back.

Once he'd found his balance, Zar began blowing the dust and cobwebs off the arrows sticking out of the quiver slung around her shoulder. He pushed his little lungs to their capacity until he was lightheaded.

"Do you even know how to work this piece of equipment?" he asked.

Lenore side-eyed him.

"It's a fair question. Vlad provides the meat for your people, so I—"

"So you assumed I don't know how to use a bow?" Her pointed glare was quite sharp.

"Well..."

After a few wobbly steps down a decline, Lenore said quietly, "I've never used one."

He squeaked. "I knew it!"

"It can't be that hard!"

Balthazar rolled his eyes.

"I can feel you rolling your eyes."

"You cannot."

"Can too."

He huffed.

They rode deeper into the snowy woods under the bat's direction, bickering about nonsense. When they came to an area just shy of the marker where Vlad left his offerings, Balthazar told her to head east.

"The clearing is just up ahead. Be quiet or you'll scare away the deer."

She flicked him off her shoulder.

"Hey!"

Her playful grin eventually had Balthazar chuckling. They were both tightly wound, and the fiery farm girl had a way of helping loosen him up. From what he could remember of his youth, his sister had been similar. Always picking on him but there to defend her youngest brother against the older ones when they tried to do the same. He often wondered what happened to his family after he'd been captured by the witch, but the void Vlad had filled in his heart was slowly making room for the girl.

When they approached the clearing, she slid off the mule and tied him to a tree.

"I'm going to scope it out," Balthazar said. "Don't even think about leaving."

"Why the hell would I leave?"

She was growing on him, but his guard was still up. "You have your mule. You could bolt as soon as I leave, head back home or go to Shademoss, like you want, leaving the count to die and me to watch."

She scoffed. "Do you think so little of me that I would do that? He's dying because of me! I would never leave him in the state he's in. How dare you accuse me of something so awful."

Balthazar shrank from her tone. He'd clearly offended her and struggled to find his words. "I'm just looking out—"

"Looking out for your friend. I know." Her jaw was clenched so tight he could see the muscle. Lenore turned her back to him, wordlessly fussing with the bow.

He would apologize later. Emotions were heightened and they didn't have time to waste.

Balthazar took off and continued east. He and Vlad came here often, as there was a wide section of river where animals always lingered. As expected, a healthy family of deer stood at the water's edge. Vlad always tried to go for animals in pain or near the end of their lifespan, but this was a desperate situation. They couldn't be picky.

He flew back and heard Lenore before he saw her. She cursed as an arrow bounced back in the bow, going nowhere.

"God-damned thing!" She snatched another from the quiver.

"You really need to work on that mouth of yours. Very unlady-like."

She nocked the arrow. "That's your concern right now?"

"Are you holding it right?"

"I don't know. Am I?"

Balthazar landed on a branch. "How should I know? Vlad doesn't use weapons."

Her head whipped around. "You're almost as old as him. You mean to tell me in all these years you've never seen someone hunt out here?"

"I didn't pay attention to how they held a bow! That information is not important to me."

"Ugh." Lenore aimed at the tree. "You're no help."

"Chastise me all you want, but it won't help our situation."

She kept her focus on the tree and pulled the bow back. Lenore loosed the arrow and missed completely.

He sighed. "This is going to be impossible."

Determination to prove him wrong settled into her features as she nocked another arrow.

"Okay, now focus," Balthazar said.

"I know that."

"Well, it didn't seem like it."

"Do you want to try?"

He kept quiet.

"That's what I thought. Now, let me do this." With a petty flick of her hair, Lenore widened her stance and slowly raised the bow. She took a deep breath, in and out. This time, her arrow hit the tree.

A cocky smile burst across her face. "Ha! Told you!" She found her mark, albeit a bit high and right.

"Good. Just make sure you hit the animal next time." Zar took flight. "Follow me. There's deer this way. Hopefully they're still there."

They left Marty tied and headed for the river, arriving a few minutes later. Lenore crept through the trees, using the thick firs for cover.

Balthazar landed nearby, careful not to make a sound. "If you miss," he whispered, "they'll all scatter. It could be hours until we find another animal this size. Vlad doesn't have that kind of time."

The cockiness slid from her face as resolution took its place. They were here for Vlad and their quarrels could wait. Lenore slowed her breathing and locked her eyes onto the target—a buck directly ahead oblivious to their presence.

"Take your time," Zar whispered.

With the river as a dampener to their sounds, the shuffle to get into the right position the nock of her arrow went unheard. The buck continued grazing, turning slightly so its chest was facing them. A perfect shot.

Lenore's posture was rigid as she drew the bow back.

They'd only have one shot at this.

A deep breath. Then another.

The buck's head snapped up.

"Now!" he wanted to scream. "Before he runs away!"

Time hinged on a single moment.

The whoosh of an arrow sounded and the buck dropped to the ground.

Balthazar let out a shriek of happiness as the rest of the deer fled up the mountain.

"I did it!" Lenore took off running, not bothering to wait for him. The quiver smacked against her back as she went, carefully stepping across the river stones as Balthazar flew overhead.

She dropped next to the dead buck and turned the quiver upside down, letting a small knife and multiple glass jars they'd brought slide out.

Watching Lenore rest the buck's head on her thigh, hold the jar under its neck, then slit its throat and catch the blood pouring out made him realize that without her, Vlad would certainly die. If he hadn't perished while they'd been gone.

The thought made him sick.

"What's wrong? Can't handle the sight of what you consume?" she jested.

"It's not that. I just feel...useless. I wouldn't have been able to do any of this." Guilt lodged itself in his throat for what he'd said to her. "I shouldn't have accused you of taking off and leaving us. I'm sorry. It's just difficult admitting you are of more use to the count than I."

"You are his best friend, Zar. You do plenty for him just by existing. Can you imagine what a century of being truly alone would have done to him?"

Balthazar considered this. "I'm just realizing how important other people are for him. There's only so much I can do, and I hate admitting that."

Lenore capped one of the jars once it was full. Blood soaked her dress, but she wasn't fazed. She held another jar under the buck's neck and collected its blood.

"You and I have something in common."

He cocked his head. "How so?"

"I haven't wanted to admit the same thing to myself. The reason I snap at you and Vlad sometimes, and the reason I've done the same to people back home, is because the last thing I want to be thought of is incapable. I don't have much to my name in this world, but I do have my pride. If I can't do something on my own, then what use am I?"

Her throat bobbed like she was straining not to let him see how much other's opinions actually affected her. Balthazar didn't know the workings of the human mind, but sitting with her now, he understood that she wasn't so different from him. It didn't matter that they weren't the same species. Pride could affect anyone.

He chuckled. "Maybe that's why you and I always bicker. We're too alike for our own good."

She chuckled and capped the second jar. "Something I actually agree with you on."

There was a mutual acceptance of one another in that moment. An understanding. As Balthazar watched her work, he wondered if he'd ever find acceptance with his own species. The desire to belong to his own kind rekindled the need to connect with other bats. Once

Vlad was safe and healthy, perhaps he would venture back to the cave.

"Do you think this is enough?" she asked.

"Two full jars should do. We need to go. It'll be dark soon."

There was no time to drag the buck to the marker and leave it for her people to retrieve. They needed to get back to the castle.

Lenore rode at a brisk pace with Balthazar flying ahead, leading the way.

After putting Marty in his stall, they rushed inside. Balthazar's heart pounded when he saw Vlad lying right where they left him, sweating profusely and pale as death as tremors racked his body.

"Oh, God." Lenore rushed to his side. She threw the blankets off and stuffed another pillow under his head. He was still breathing, but barely.

Zar rolled one of the blood jars toward her with his nose. "Hurry!"

"I'm trying!"

When she uncapped the jar and brought it toward his mouth, Vlad's eyes flew open.

Eyes black as midnight Balthazar had only seen once before. A chill shot down his spine.

# 13

## Vlad

Vlad was ravenous. There was food in front of him. A thrumming heartbeat under a sea of long, yellow hair.

Something small smacked him in the face. A creature. A bat. *Food.*

The furry thing yelled something Vlad couldn't distinguish that made the blonde animal run.

The beast within him sprang into motion. He snarled, canines throbbing, ready to puncture anything that would bring him sustenance.

The bat cut him off, flapping around his face. He tried to swat it away, but the creature was relentless. Vlad made a guttural noise similar to words, but not quite. It was a primal sound of necessity. The need to devour.

When the bat came at him again, Vlad swung hard. Anger welled up inside him when he missed. He was so damn hungry, and the smell of blood somewhere drove him into a frenzy.

*Where was it? Where was he?* Shapes blurred as he whirled, but the environment was like looking out a dirty window. Nothing concrete or tangible.

"Sire! Sire!" the bat kept saying.

Vlad snarled, not knowing what it meant.

Small pink eyes got directly in his face. "Vlad Dracula!"

A flicker of recognition. He'd seen this bat before. Heard that name.

"Sire, you must feed! Now!"

*What was the creature saying?*

Vlad pressed his hands to his temples, head pounding. *Where was all the blood he smelled?*

The bat darted away and Vlad followed out of instinct.

"Sire, here!"

Someone had called him that before. *Was it his name?*

His nostrils flared. The tangy scent of blood carried him toward a large fire set inside stones. Another strange sound came out of him seeing a container full of blood.

The first jar went down so quickly he hardly registered it. As Vlad drank from the second, the room changed from indistinguishable fragments into pieces he could make out. Rugs on the floor. Furniture. A chess set. Paintings on the wall. *Who were those people in the portraits?*

"Sire?" a timid voice said. The bat from earlier crawled toward him.

Vlad licked the blood off his lips, groaning his ecstasy. "I recognize you." The voice that came out of him was husky. Gravelly. Not his own.

"Yes. I am Balthazar."

Vlad frowned. He thought he remembered seeing something white around the bat's neck earlier but it wasn't there anymore.

The bat came a little closer. "I'm your friend. We play chess together. We live here."

Vlad looked around the room. He went back to drinking the blood as the frenzy within him calmed. He realized he was sitting on his knees, jar cupped tight between both hands.

This wasn't how he normally fed.

"I am Balthazar. Your friend."

"Balthazar," he parroted. The word felt familiar on his tongue.

The bat nodded. "And you are Vlad Dracula. This is your castle. You are the last heir of the royal family."

*Those must have been the people in the portraits.*

Vlad finished the jar and inhaled deeply. Delicious. A warm feeling started in his innards, and he closed his eyes, smiling while licking a line of blood from the corner of his mouth. Calm satiation spread to his limbs and grounded him, bringing a flood of memories forth.

A ballroom.

A witch.

Torture.

A bat.

Sorrow.

A woman.

Vlad's eyes flew open.

Balthazar sat on the ground, body tense.

"Why are you looking at me like that, Zar?"

His friend blew out a breath. "Thank God. I thought I'd lost you."

"Lost me how?" Vlad became aware of his tight grip around the jar and frowned. "Why is there blood in here?" He tasted it on his tongue. "Did I drink this?"

"Yes, sire. It's a long story, but you were attacked by wolves and lost a lot of blood. And because you hadn't fed, you went into bloodlust when you woke. I haven't seen you like that since your early years."

Vlad remembered. He'd only lost control once and recalled a similar feeling. A near uncontrollable urge to consume blood. A loss of self-awareness and a mind fraught with revolting thoughts and sensations.

Dread made his heart sink. "I didn't hurt you, did I?"

"No, sire. You did not."

"Thank heavens." Vlad checked himself over, realizing his chest was bare. His shirt and vest lay in a bloody heap nearby, cut down the middle. His fingers found a stitched line along his shoulder, though there was no pain. Both shoes had been removed and there were more stitches on the backside of his ankle, but no pain when he touched the wound.

*Who had done this to him?*

Balthazar said something, but Vlad's attention went to the jars. "How did you get this blood?"

"As I was saying, sire, you didn't hurt me, but you did frighten someone else."

"Who?"

"The person who got that blood for you."

Vlad didn't understand.

"Lenore."

His eyes nearly bulged out of his head. The animal with the blonde hair hadn't been an animal at all. It was her. "Oh, God! Please tell me I didn't hurt her." He was going to vomit.

"You did not lay a finger on her," Balthazar reassured him. "But she did see you in your...state. She's upstairs in her room."

Vlad cradled his face in his hands. He had never hated himself more than he did in that moment. "What have I done?"

"You haven't done anything to her. That's what's important."

He shook his head. "She'll never speak to me again. She probably scaled the castle, took her mule, and left."

"I doubt that, sire. It's much too high a jump, even for someone as headstrong as her." Balthazar chuckled, but Vlad couldn't find it in him to laugh.

"I've ruined everything."

"Then go fix it."

"I don't know how. How do I explain why I am the way I am when I don't even know myself?"

Zar rested a wing on his hand. "Perhaps, start by explaining *how* you became this way. You wanted her to know you. Here's your chance."

His stomach was in knots. "She won't want to know me now, but I'll try. Will you go with me and speak to her first? She may not even want to see me."

"Of course."

Vlad followed his friend in silence. He stopped by his room and changed into a new pair of clothes, forgoing his usual formal wear and choosing black pants and a simple white dress shirt instead. He gathered the lavender he'd cut for Lenore's room when he went out to find her breakfast, hoping it would act as a peace offering.

Shame at what he'd become and losing himself in bloodlust made his throat tighten. The closer they got to her room, the more his hands began to sweat. Vlad smoothed his hair back. "Zar," he whispered. "How do I look?"

After a few directions from his friend on how to clean up his appearance, Vlad straightened his sleeves and stood up straight. "Okay," he whispered. "I'm ready."

Balthazar approached her door. "Miss?"

"Yes?" a shaky voice said. "Are you all right, Zar?"

"I'm fine. I have the count with me and he would like to speak to you. He's all better now."

Silence.

Vlad's heart ripped. She would never give him a chance to explain. Not that he deserved one.

"Okay..." Lenore's acceptance was music to his ears, even if it was reluctant.

He listened to her pad to the door. At the turn of the knob, Vlad froze. *What was he going to say? How would he explain himself?*

Lenore cautiously opened the door and peeked out. She looked at Zar, then wide, green eyes flicked to him.

The smile that bloomed felt awkward on his face. Like it hung too high on one side.

She disappeared behind the door. "Come in."

Zar gave him a nod of encouragement. "I'll wait downstairs."

Vlad stood at the threshold clutching the bundle of lavender. "Please give me a chance to explain. Please don't run away," he muttered. The count took a deep breath and entered the room.

# 14

## VLAD

Lenore stood by the bed, fingers twisting in her skirt. She was back to wearing her own clothes and not the ones he'd lent her.

Taking it as a sign that she would be leaving soon, Vlad tried to prepare himself for the conversation ahead. "Would you like me to leave the door open or close it?" he asked.

"You can close it."

He hated how timid her voice was. As if she spoke too loudly it might thrust him back into his former state. Vlad stayed on the opposite side of the room. "I brought you some lavender."

She gave him a small smile. "Thank you."

He set the bundle on the desk and awkwardly smoothed the front of his shirt a few times. "Lenore, I—"

"Your eyes are red again." She kept herself angled away from him. Body rigid as a deer when it knew a predator was watching.

Vlad did the only thing he could think of to make himself appear less intimidating. He dropped to his knees and sat back on his heels. He kept his gaze on the floor, too ashamed to look her in the eye.

"If you'll allow me, I would like to explain what happened, why it happened, and reassure you that it will never happen again."

"You don't have to kneel."

He didn't dare look up. Not without her permission. "Yes, I do. Because I must beg your forgiveness for the man I became."

The longer her silence continued, the more his eyes began to burn.

"Will you promise to tell me everything?" she eventually asked. "No lies?"

"Yes," he said immediately.

"Vlad."

He looked up.

Lenore sat on the left side of the bed and patted the empty space beside her. "Come lay down."

He tentatively approached.

"You can put your head in my lap."

*She was going to let him get close. Not shun him away.* His heart leapt. Vlad had to angle himself diagonally so he could fit entirely on the bed. He lowered his head onto Lenore's lap and apprehensively made eye contact with her.

She encouraged him with a smile. "Tell me everything."

Clasping both hands together and resting them on his stomach, Vlad focused on the ceiling, wondering where to start.

Lenore brushed a piece of hair back from his forehead. A movement he could only remember his mother doing once. Not in comfort, but to check him over to see if he'd lied again about falling out of a tree.

The gentleness of her fingers combing through his hair tore a pathetic whimper out of him. "You don't have to do that. I don't deserve your kindness."

"Yes, you do."

Vlad wanted to wrap her in his arms and never let go. Thank her for not fleeing and for letting him be with her now. His eyes watered with grateful tears. He looked back at the ceiling and let the affectionate fingers running through his hair coax the truth out of him.

"I suppose I should start with what everyone wants to know. What happened the night of my family ball one-hundred-and-forty years ago."

He traced the imperfections in the stone ceiling with his eyes, letting the memories he'd fought so hard to bury come back.

"I remember it was snowing. The drive outside was packed with carriages and people dressed in their finery. My father put me on coat check duty, but a fourteen-year-old boy can only do that for so long before he gets bored."

The sound of Lenore's quiet chuckle made the words start to come easier as he relaxed into the bed.

"So I snuck away, trying to hide from my mother's eyesight, which proved quite easy with how many people were in the Great Hall. Nobles from all over the country were here to celebrate my father's ascension in rank. All the silver had been polished to the highest shine. Took the staff an entire week to do it all. Every crystal on the chandelier was dusted, every floorboard scrubbed twice over."

So colorful. So full of sound and life. A smile bloomed on his face at the memory of what once was. "You should have seen this place back then. It sure was beautiful."

His smile faded as the rest of the night came into clarity. "I remember I was planning a sneak attack on the dessert tray when a woman gasped so loud she stopped the bustle of entire the room. I couldn't see what everyone was looking at, so I moved closer to the dais near my parents. My father pointed at the foot of the steps where a hunched old woman stood in rags with her face hidden."

The witch's face, her wrinkles and horrible, sickly-colored eyes, haunted him. Sometimes he could recall her stench, even in his nightmares. Sulfur and noxious fumes he'd come to know later as the smells of her vile potions. He should have hid. Should have watched from afar instead of going to his mother. Maybe everything would have turned out differently.

"You don't have to continue. We can stop," Lenore said.

Vlad didn't realize how tense he was. He put Lenore's free hand on his chest and squeezed her fingers. "I want to tell you. I just might need to go slow."

She squeezed his fingers back, looking down at him with that beautiful face of hers. "Of course. Take all the time you need."

He couldn't help but stare at her. At the way loose strands of wavy golden hair dangled by her cheeks. The soft flutter of her lashes. Her moss-colored eyes. A heart that didn't hate him and ears willing to listen. He would never take her for granted.

"You truly are the kindest person I have ever known," he said.

"Don't let Balthazar hear you say that. Even though he's not a person, I'm sure he'll fight me to take back that number one spot."

The two chuckled, and Vlad had never felt so at ease with another. He was falling hard, and if Lenore only wanted friendship and never saw him as anything more than a pit stop on the way to start her new life, he would accept that. But he knew if she ever let him kiss her that Lenore would have his heart for as long as she wanted. It didn't matter that she'd only been in the castle for a brief time. His heart was done for.

Vlad snuggled deeper into her lap and she returned to combing through his hair. "My father confronted the woman who had come to the castle without invitation. When she removed her hood, we all saw her for what she was. A witch. Eyes turned an unnatural yellow green from the use of dark magic. I had only read about witches and didn't think they were real, so I wiggled out of my mother's grip to get a better look, and that's when she spotted me. I spent years revisiting that night wondering if I was the one that secured my fate."

*It's not your fault,* Balthazar repeated over the years. *You can't blame yourself for what happened.*

Some days, Vlad believed the words as truth. Other days, it was hard not to be crippled with shame.

"The witch demanded an offering. She wanted someone to experiment on. When my father denied her and told her to leave, she killed five of our guards with a simple lift of her bony finger and a muttered spell."

Lenore's hand tensed under his.

"She said she would kill everyone in the castle unless she was allotted one person to be allowed to leave with her. I thought her insane and looked around at everyone whispering and murmuring to one another. I didn't know what would happen, but I felt a strange tingling like I was being watched. The witch smiled with a black mouth completely void of teeth, pointed at me, and said in this awful screeching voice, 'The boy.' I was the only child there and she picked me because I was small and thought I'd be the easiest to control."

The feel of the woman's clammy hands on him. Her rancid breath. Her surprising strength. *He never stood a chance against her.*

"I'm so sorry, Vlad." Lenore swiped her thumb along his hand. The softest movement that made him unsure how to react.

"I don't mean to be so stiff, I've just never received this kind of comfort," he said with painful admission.

"Even from your mother?"

Vlad shifted uncomfortably. "Well, that's the next part of the story. My father was outraged that the witch killed his guards, so he threatened her with death if she didn't leave. She cackled this hideous sound and pulled what looked like a pile of glittering sand from her pocket.

"When she blew on the sand, it traveled in a line seemingly of its own accord. The royals on the receiving end of the dust choked and their veins turned black as they fell to the floor. Dead. My father quieted down after that.

"But the witch insisted on me, and after a short deliberation between my parents, my mother gave me up."

Lenore gasped. "She just gave you to the witch?"

He nodded. "My father said he and my mother could make more children. His concerns for having an heir to the family line far outweighed his love for me."

"God, that's awful. I can't even imagine…"

"My father wasn't always that way. I spent many hours in his study while he worked. Being quiet and just watching. I don't know what happened between my childhood and when I became a teenager. I don't know what changed his mind about loving me."

Vlad's throat tightened, but the light touch of nails against his scalp urged him to continue. "Leaving the castle was a blur. Protests came from the nobles, the servants, and from people I didn't even know. They put up more of a fight than my own kin. I screamed at my parents as the witch dragged me outside in her impossibly strong grip. I told them my life was not some bargaining chip, but my pleas went unanswered. At least my father had the decency to appear upset. Far better than the indifference coming from my mother."

His mother's eyes deadened as she watched her only son being taken into the night. *How could someone who birthed him be so cold and unloving?* Vlad stopped asking that question years ago.

"Leaving the castle wasn't as painful as what came after." Flashes of his life stuck in the witch's hut whizzed through his mind, pausing in their worst moments.

Vlad tensed, arms tightening over his chest. He had the overwhelming sense that he was trapped. Barricaded in. He sat up, breaths coming quick.

Lenore crawled across the bed until she was in his eye-line. "It's okay. I'm right here. You're safe."

He watched her mouth the words as the tunnel vision crept in, but he couldn't get enough air down. His skin prickled with heat and dread roiled his stomach.

Lenore took his face in her hands. "Look at me, Vlad. Deep breaths. Like this."

He tried his best to mimic her movements before he succumbed to the panic.

"No one's going to hurt you. I won't let that happen."

Her soft hands on his cheeks brought Vlad back to the room they were in and not that awful place where he'd been trapped for who knows how long. The tunnel vision widened until Lenore was his sole focus.

Overcome, Vlad wrapped his arms around her, burying his face in her hair. His size dwarfed her, but she squeezed him in a way that said she wouldn't let go until he did.

Tears burst from him like a geyser as Vlad held on to the woman who couldn't possibly understand, but the empathy radiating from her warmed his half-dead heart. There were no words. Only sobs racking Vlad's body, but he didn't dare let go. He'd been given a gift, so he clung to that gift until the tempest inside him steadied.

He pulled back to see Lenore crying too. Vlad gently wiped away her tears with his thumbs. "I used to call out to God to save me from my torment. He never answered me back then, but I know now that you, Lenore, can only be someone heaven-sent."

Her bottom lip wobbled.

He let her dry his tears, leaning into her caring touch. "You are a gift, Lenore. A blessing to my weary soul. Even if you are only a brief star in my sky and you choose to move along, having you here has brought me more peace than I have ever known."

She cradled his face in her hands. "I don't want to move along."

He sucked in a breath. "What?"

Her watery gaze moved from his eyes to his mouth. "I want to stay. At least for a little while. If you'll have me."

His heart nearly exploded with joy.

She leaned in closer, Vlad doing the same. Anticipation hung between them with the charge of a summer lightning storm.

Lenore's fingers moved to his hair. Her chest heaved, lips parting as they stared into each other's eyes. He'd never kissed anyone, but he wasn't worried about being clumsy. He just needed her.

"Please," he said desperately. Yearning for anything she would give him. Anything at all.

When she pressed her soft lips to his, Vlad's dark sky burst into stars.

# 15

# VLAD

Lenore's velvety lips caressed his, but it was the transformation happening inside he knew would alter him forever. There was no going back from this. From her.

When her tongue slipped into his mouth, he groaned. It felt strange at first, but the more their tongues tangled, the more his arousal heightened. He crawled over Lenore until her back hit the sheets. She pulled at his waist until the soft contours of her body met the large muscles of his.

Vlad braced both arms beside her head. "I don't want to squish you."

"You won't." She opened her legs, bracketing his hips with supple thighs begging to be touched, saying in a sultry whisper, "Give me all of you."

When his erection pressed firmly against her stomach, the raspy noise that came out of Vlad rattled in his throat. He kissed her deeply, learning the give and take of their lips moving together. Large hands roamed her curves as the fabric of her skirt bunched in his needy fingers. Vlad palmed her breast, exploring as she arched her back and groaned into his mouth. With one hand at the nape of his neck and the other gripping his hip tight, Lenore kept their bodies in a tight, warm embrace.

Vlad wanted to devour her. To drown in the depths of her loveliness. Her flushed cheeks were so adorable, and the feel of her against him...He couldn't describe it in any way other than 'divine bliss'. "God, Lenore. You're so beautiful," he whispered against her mouth.

She answered with a sweltering kiss, searing him with desire. Lenore unbuttoned his shirt and lightly dragged her nails down his abdomen. All the wounds on his body had rapidly healed thanks to the blood she'd gotten for him, and Vlad wanted to express his gratitude for her care in the most physical, primal way.

He would never get tired of her touching him. Kissing him. Hell, just looking at him. Vlad began exploring her neck and chest with his mouth, unconvinced he wasn't hallucinating and that this was actually happening.

To feel another's touch like this. To yearn for them whole-heartedly. How would he ever return to life after Lenore? He didn't care that he'd only known her a short time. She was imprinted on his soul.

Vlad slid his hand under her shirt, exposing her midriff, his uneven breaths fanning her hair. He was so distracted by the glorious reveal of more of her skin that he didn't hear the soft knock at the door.

"Not now, Zar," he grumbled before planting his lips back on hers. Every sound she made had him wanting to discover all the noises in her repertoire.

"I wouldn't interrupt if it wasn't important," Zar said a bit tentatively.

Vlad fisted the sheets, jaw clenched.

Lenore pulled him closer. "Don't leave."

He kissed her again and had to force himself not to continue. "Let me see what he wants and I'll be right back." He stomped toward the door and yanked it open halfway, shielding Lenore from view. "Yes?"

Balthazar whispered, "There are torches in the woods. The humans are further north than the marker. I think they're wondering why they haven't received any offerings in two days."

Fear shot through his body. The last time people with torches came they tried to set fire to his home. "I'll be right down," he said softly. "Stay with Lenore. Neither of you go outside while I'm gone."

"Yes, sire."

Vlad shut the door and returned to the bed, leaning over Lenore. God, he wanted to climb under the sheets with her so badly. "I have to go check on something, but I'll be back shortly."

She trailed her fingers up and down his forearm, green eyes glittering in the candlelight. "Is everything all right?"

He didn't want her to worry, so he faked a smile. "Everything is fine. I've just been lacking on doing my perimeter checks and I just want to make sure you stay safe. Sometimes animals like to wander too close. I'll check on Marty while I'm out."

When he kissed her neck, she squirmed and giggled. "That tickles!"

After more kissing, he pried himself away from her with more restraint than even his bloodlust required. "Keep the bed warm for me and I'll be back as soon as I can."

She pulled the covers up to her chin. "I guess I'll stay in this lavish castle, in this massive bed waiting for an incredibly attractive man to come back to me." The back of her hand went to her forehead as she feigned discomfort. "Oh, however shall I manage?"

Vlad chuckled and gave her his most proper bow. "Your comfort is all I care about, madam. Enjoy every minute of it." When he made it into the hall, Balthazar was waiting on the banister.

"How many?" Vlad asked, hurrying down the stairs.

"I counted six torches. Less than a quarter mile north of the marker."

He glanced out a window. Small bits of flame moved in and out of the trees in the distance. Since it wasn't actively snowing, Vlad donned his simple black cloak and left the hat and gloves behind. "Lock the door. Don't let anyone in."

"Certainly. I will look after the girl. Be careful, my friend."

With an affirming nod, the count stepped into the cold night. The moon kept hidden, as if it didn't want to witness what he anticipated. He hurried through the shadowy forest, feet barely making a sound as his superior speed carried him down the mountain, closing in on the humans.

Vlad hid behind a cluster of firs and watched a group of six men tromp through the snow. Each carried a bow and two were armed with additional axes. Dirty faces matched their raggedy clothes, and even upwind he could smell their stench. Vlad turned up his nose. None of them would have been fit for Lenore. No wonder she wanted to leave.

"Not a one of us has seen that fucker," a pudgy, older man said. "My grandpa's the one that made the deal, so how do we know it's even the same monster leaving us food?"

His jaw clenched at the derogatory word.

A man with a thick red beard led the pack. He spat on the ground. "You dumb bag of rocks. You think there are two things in these woods that can drain an animal of all its blood? It's the same demon that's preyed on this mountain for centuries. I know it."

The portly man spoke again. "I'm just saying, there could be more than one monster helping it. Surely devils travel in packs."

A teenage boy chimed in. "You really think there's more than one?"

"Only one way to find out," red beard said with a determined look on his face, grip tightening around the axe.

Vlad's heart thudded. He wouldn't let them anywhere near his home.

"Maybe we shouldn't go to the castle," the boy said. "Maybe we should just leave it alone."

Red beard said, "We aren't gonna figure shit out standing here scratching our asses. We're going to the castle. Any man that's too much of a coward can turn back now."

Vlad solidified his plan as they approached. One he'd mulled over many times in case a moment like this ever came. He stepped into their line of sight a safe distance away.

"Gentlemen," the count said in his most polished voice.

They froze, necks craning to look at him.

Vlad spread his arms wide. "I mean no harm, I—"

One of the men quickly loosed an arrow. Vlad dodged it with ease. He went to explain himself again, but another arrow whizzed by.

His father had always been cool and collected in the face of conflict. The man's one good quality Vlad tried to emulate now. "There's no need for that. I'm just here to talk."

"Monster!" Red beard shouted, axe raised.

Vlad bit back his anger. "I have been feeding your kind for over a century. Tell me, good sir, would a monster do such a thing?"

The men glanced at one another, but none said a word. The moon peeked out from the clouds, highlighting their wide, terrified eyes.

The plump man spoke. "You...talk."

Vlad clasped his hands in front of him as a peaceful gesture. "Yes. I heard you all speaking on your way here. I am the one who made a deal with your grandfather all those years ago. There is no other but me."

Red beard blinked. "He did not speak of a man your...size. He said you were a gangly limbed, skinny savage with blood-filled eyes and fangs."

The teenage boy swallowed. "You got the red eyes and fangs right."

Vlad had learned his lesson with Lenore and made sure to keep still so as not to spook the men. If this was to end amicably, he needed to come off less threatening. "I apologize for the forgotten deliveries. I have been ill."

"Bullshit. A monster like you *is* the sickness."

"Have I not held up my end of the bargain all these years? Surely you can forgive two days of missing meals over the course of thousands."

A puny man in the back spoke. "We've left you and your castle alone in exchange for food. You owe us!"

Vlad exhaled heavily through his nose. They truly were the incapable hunters Lenore said they were. Not that he ever doubted her. "Without me, you would be forced to hunt on your own. You rely on me to be your provider."

Multiple arrows were nocked and pointed Vlad's way. Red beard held up a fist like he controlled his men with it. "Then provide."

When he widened his stance, the men took a step back. All except red beard.

"Do you really think you all could stand against me?" Vlad added more menace to his voice, struggling to maintain his diplomacy. "You saw how quickly I caught your arrows. Do you think you could get to me before I stopped you?"

They seemed to think better of their plan and lowered their weapons.

"I would like to negotiate our terms," Vlad said.

"Which are?" red beard asked.

"That our agreement be dissolved. We've had peace for years, and I want nothing more than for it to continue, but I will not be your butcher anymore. You must learn to provide for yourselves. I am not looking to instigate violence. I simply wish for us to go our separate ways."

"And why would we accept this new agreement of yours when we lose?"

With each word out of red beard's mouth, Vlad understood why Lenore was fed up with her community if they were all this reliant and useless. "I should think men would want to be self-sufficient."

"You are one man. We are a village of many. With all of us standing against you, surely we could take your life and your castle."

"That would be unwise." Even a small, underlying threat felt unnatural coming out of his mouth.

Red beard glared. "We do not accept your terms. Your red eyes and death-toned skin don't scare me. All men have weaknesses." He pointed his axe at Vlad. "I will find out what yours are."

"You do not wish to test my capabilities," Vlad warned. "Be gone and leave me be, and I shall do the same."

Red beard discreetly flicked a finger, but Vlad saw it. Without taking his eyes off the villagers, he stuck his arm out and caught the arrow that came at him from somewhere deeper in the forest. Vlad snapped it in half and bared his fangs. "I gave you a chance."

He lunged and grabbed red beard by the collar, lifting him up with one hand as the man kicked wildly. He didn't want to resort to violence, but Balthazar and Lenore were his responsibility, so he would make sure the pitiful people of Newthorn wouldn't dare try to approach his home again.

He would only do this once. For his friends. He leaned in close to the man choking and pleading in his grip. "You want a monster?"

Red beard's eyes blew wide.

"I'll give you a monster."

When Vlad bared his fangs and acted like he was going to bite the man, red beard let out a garbled scream.

Vlad tossed him into the others and they fell to the ground in a heap. He strategically scanned the woods and caught sight of the archer who shot at him fleeing down the mountain.

Good riddance.

The count gripped the sides of his cloak and raised them high. A tactic animals did to make themselves appear larger. "You ever come back here, and I'll kill you all! Mount your heads above my mantle and use your skin for curtains!"

A bit theatrical, but it worked. The men scrambled to get up, tripping over each other.

Vlad showed his fangs again. "I shall drain every last person of blood and descend on your village like never-ending night!" Needing to make sure he drove his point home, Vlad appeared in front of red beard and deepened his voice as much as he could. "Do I make myself clear?"

"Y-yes. We'll never come back."

"Good." The count vanished and reappeared up the mountain, laughing as the group frantically ran down the mountain on shaky legs.

On the way back home, the hilarity of his ridiculous threats morphed into something that caused a queasiness in his stomach. He had to force the bile back down from having to become someone he never wanted to be. Frightening people was not something that made him feel bigger or like more of a man. Violence was not in his nature, and he never wanted to resort to it. He didn't want anyone to be able to put stock in the word 'monster', and now they surely would.

Head hung low, Vlad stepped inside the castle and hung up his cloak. He heard Balthazar and Lenore and followed their voices to her room. The door was halfway open, so he peeked inside.

Lenore held a sewing needle in one hand and a small piece of white fabric in the other. "If you weren't wriggling around so much, I wouldn't have poked you!"

"If you actually knew what you were doing, you wouldn't have stabbed me!"

When she reached for him, Balthazar hopped off the bed. "Missed me!"

Vlad covered his mouth so they wouldn't hear him laughing.

"Get back here and let me finish this damn collar!"

He realized that's what was missing from around Balthazar's neck. The item he'd noticed after his bloodlust had settled. Vlad must have torn it off him somehow.

Balthazar had kept him from getting to her and Vlad had ruined his collar in the process. Yet here she was, fixing a new one for him, stitching Vlad's wrongdoings back together for his friend that had put himself in harm's way to protect her.

The count watched the friends he cared most about chase each other around the room as Lenore tried to fit Zar for the collar she'd sewn. He knew at that moment that if keeping them safe and happy came at the cost of having to turn into a monster occasionally, he would gladly pay it.

For them.

# 16

## LENORE

She tried to grab Balthazar and missed. "Would you sit down so I can measure you? You stubborn, furry ferret!"

That got his attention.

"How dare you reduce me to a rat of a creature!"

Lenore paused to catch her breath. "You're a fast little fucker."

"Again, with the language, Lenore! Do you have any idea how many fine, respectable people have walked these halls? This was a bedroom for visiting duchesses, for God's sake."

She chuckled. *He was so easy to rile.* "Come on. Say a bad word. I dare you."

Balthazar landed on top of the armoire so she couldn't reach him. "I will not."

"Come on. Just one."

He turned up his nose in that stuffy way of his. "No."

"I've been trying to get him to for years," a deep voice said. Vlad strolled into the room, one hand in his pocket and the other casually gesturing to his friend.

Her whole body tingled at the sight of him. So polished and poised. Handsome and debonair. And the taste of his tongue as he'd kissed her...

"But Zar has always been more refined than us humans." Vlad's dazzling smile nearly brought Lenore to her knees. He'd left in the middle of a passionate kiss, making her eyes drift to his mouth. When he caught her staring, she quickly looked away.

Balthazar descended from his moral high horse and landed on the desk. "Everything ship-shape, sire?"

"Nothing to be concerned about."

"Good. Good."

She had the sense this was no perimeter check, as Vlad had called it, but he appeared unscathed and in good spirits. In fact, he looked better than ever. Chest puffed out like he was proud.

"I'm glad you're all right," Lenore blurted out. Her fingers rung in her skirt, heart beating rapidly. How quickly the count had gone from frightening to delectable. Against her better judgement, she'd let him and his fangs get close, though never fearing what he might do. There was only desire and the need for more.

"I'm perfectly fine, thank you. What happened while I was gone?"

They both talked over one another, Balthazar trying to paint her in the wrong.

Vlad laughed deeply. He was so beautiful. Skin the color of marble but a heart as soft as the inside of a rose. *How could his parents ever give him up?* Listening to him detail the horrible events of the night that altered his life nearly broke her heart in half.

"Good thing I came back before there was any bloodshed. Come now, Zar. Lenore is only trying to help."

The bat squeaked his disapproval. "She needs etiquette classes and a steady sewing hand."

She rolled her eyes. "Don't be such a baby."

Zar stuck his tongue out.

It was quiet for a moment before all three of them burst into a fit. No evidence of the cold, drab castle she'd encountered upon arrival existed. There was warm candlelight, hearty laughter, and a carefree ease between the three of them. A place that felt more like a home than the one Lenore had lived in all her life.

When they'd settled down, the hunger in Vlad's gaze returned, setting her skin ablaze from the intensity of his eyes raking her over.

After a few seconds of awkward silence, Balthazar excused himself. "I don't want my beauty sleep interrupted. Do try to keep it down."

"Okay, off to bed, friend," Vlad said quickly, blushing and ushering the bat out of the room.

Zar chuckled as he flew out into the hall and the door was shut behind him.

"When you blush, you blush purple," Lenore said. "Actually, more of a lilac color."

Vlad touched his cheek. "I do?"

Seeing him nervously start to rub the back of his neck made her snicker. "It's cute."

His eyes darted to the bed. "I uhh...I don't know if you want to...umm..."

He was so sweet. So innocent. Lenore sauntered over to him. "I would love to continue." She stood on her toes and pulled his face down to hers, planting her lips on his. Vlad's large hands found her waist, and it wasn't long before their kissing turned needy.

She unbuttoned his shirt and pushed it off his body, letting him shrug out of it on his own. Lenore frantically untied the strings on the back of her dress, loosening them the best she could. She wanted all of him, desperately. He deserved everything and she wanted to be the one to give it to him.

Vlad stood bare chested and in black trousers. His stomach muscles were slightly visible, and a dark trail of hair ran from his navel down, down, down.

She couldn't stand not touching him. Lenore closed the distance between them and jumped into his arms, smashing her lips to his.

He effortlessly carried her to the bed, stepping out of his pants along the way.

A madness took over her as Lenore clung to him like tree sap, never wanting to rid herself of the way he felt against her. His smooth lips and slightly clumsy kisses were so endearing that all concern for him ever harming her disappeared.

Foolhardy, but she didn't care.

He laid her on the bed and stepped back, standing only in his undershorts looking like some kind of god lost to the history books.

"Men don't look like you, Vlad. You're unreal, she said from her place lying on the bed. "Exquisite."

He crawled over her and smiled wide enough to show his fangs, though she was not afraid. "Compared to you, I am nothing."

"Don't sell yourself short." She helped him remove her clothing until she was lying beneath him in only a breastband and underwear. His eyes raked over her boldly, sculpted chest heaving as he ran an adoring hand along her curves.

Lenore gripped his upper body, needing to feel him on top of her. The animalistic sound that came from deep within his throat slickened the place between her legs, but she froze when her fingers met multiple, coin-sized bumps on his back.

Vlad's breathing ramped up, eyes darting around. A similar response he had earlier when mentioning the witch.

She felt further up his back, finding more bumps of varying sizes. "Did the witch give these to you?"

"I..." His breaths sounded pained. *He was panicking.*

Lenore sat up and clutched his face, trying to bring him back to reality. "Vlad, look at me. You're all right. You're safe."

He stared at her, but she didn't know if he was truly seeing her. She stroked his cheek, talking in a soothing tone. "You're in your castle. You're here with me. Everything's okay."

He nodded slowly.

"Breathe slow and deep like this." She showed him how until he began to mirror her. It took minutes, but eventually, his breathing steadied.

Lenore dropped her hands to give him some space though everything inside her said 'wrap him in your arms and hold him close.' She wanted to tell him nothing like that would ever happen to him again. Not while she was around. Unsure if the statement would be too bold, Lenore went with, "Take your time. I'll be right here."

Vlad rolled over to the other side of the bed and lied on his back, hand covering his heart. "Old memories," he said, watching the ceiling.

Lenore curled onto her side. Afraid to touch him and send him into another fit, she kept her hands to herself. "I'm here to listen if you want to talk about it."

He slipped his hand in hers, interlocking their fingers. "Those wounds are from my time in captivity, but I don't want my past to ruin this moment." He tried to kiss her but she stopped him.

"I don't think that's best right now. We can wait. I want you to feel comfortable. There's no pressure to do anything."

Vlad visibly relaxed and squeezed her hand. Soft, kind eyes met hers. "Thank you, Lenore. Thank you for bringing me back down from it."

She pushed a strand of soft midnight hair back from his forehead. "Why don't we just talk instead? Take it slow." She wanted him, badly, but his mental clarity and comfort was most important.

"I would like that."

They settled into the bed, holding hands and conversing until the candles burned low. Lenore did most of the talking, at Vlad's request. He was fascinated by her boring village life stories. Between bouts of laughter and serious moments, there was kissing. Only a little, going as slow as necessary.

By the time the moon was high in the sky, Lenore was half-draped across his body, the two of them tucked under the covers.

She drew random shapes on his chest with her finger while explaining the process of how to make bread. Vlad asked many questions, holding her as her words became few and far between.

*Contentment.* That must have been what this feeling was, Lenore thought, realizing she'd never experience it before. The last thing she remembered was Vlad kissing the top of her head and whispering something in what sounded like a very old but very beautiful language.

# 17

## VLAD

Vlad moved his knight to a vulnerable spot.

Balthazar eyed him from across the table. "A risky move, sire. Feeling daring this morning?"

He tried to hide his smirk. Though he'd slept with Lenore, he hadn't *slept* with her. His damn panic had ruined the moment.

After the long night they spent talking and learning about one another, he was grateful she had stopped it, no matter how much he wanted to continue. He needed her friendship as much as he wanted her physically.

Their conversation was intimate, and he'd still gotten to kiss her in between bouts of discussion. Each time she touched him, Vlad prayed his panic wouldn't interrupt the moment. Without control over his memories, he wasn't sure if he'd ever be able to be with her physically without it ending poorly. That is, if she even gave him another chance.

Vlad hadn't wanted to leave her bed in the morning, but he would never put his friends at risk again with his bloodlust, so he went to the woods and fed early. Without having to leave leftovers for the humans, he made it back to the castle in record time.

"Sire?"

Vlad blinked. "Sorry. What?"

The corner of Zar's lips quirked. "She's got you discombobulated."

He chuckled. "Can you blame me? I mean..." He trailed off, thinking about how long he'd watched Lenore sleep peacefully while smoothing her hair. For the first time since he'd become a vampire, Vlad didn't have to spend the night alone. Now, he was playing chess with his dearest friend in a home humans would no longer disturb with a beautiful woman upstairs. His life had never been so full of joy.

The count made his next move. "You're looking a little bare, my friend. Why not let Lenore fit you for a new collar?"

"Teach her how to properly sew like you, and I might."

"You two are stubborn, but your spats make for delightful entertainment."

Balthazar moved a bishop with his nose. "She is good for you, sire. I admit that. If Lenore decides to stay longer, I will teach her manners befitting a royal like yourself."

Vlad surveyed the board. "She asked to stay last night."

"Truly?"

He nodded. "I was delighted of course, but while I was out feeding, I thought about her dream to start a life in Shademoss. There's no opportunity for growth here. She might want to stay now, but what if she gets bored? What if she leaves?" His heart lurched.

Balthazar turned contemplative. "You make a fair point. I'm—"

"Good morning!" Lenore burst into the Great Hall with a big smile and rosy cheeks. Her long, loose waves surrounded her in a golden halo, making her truly look like the angel he'd called her last night after she'd fallen asleep.

If she did decide to leave sooner than he anticipated, Vlad didn't know how he'd ever recover.

She patted Balthazar on the head. "Good morning, Mr. Grumpy. I finished your collar." She held up the mended fabric, and though Zar looked at it skeptically, Vlad knew he was interested.

"Can I put it on you?" she asked.

"Is there a hidden pin that'll stick me?"

"Guess you'll just have to find out."

The bat dragged his eyes to Vlad. "And you call me stubborn?"

"Actually, I said you both were." He flashed Lenore a smile, delighted when she sent one back.

"Fine, I will accept the collar, miss."

"Oh, you called me 'miss'. I see I haven't completely lost your favor." Lenore wrapped the fabric around his fluffy neck, securing it with a black button, looking good as new. "A perfect fit! Back to your pretty, prissy self."

Balthazar lifted his nose. "Some of us are dignified with or without our garments."

Lenore leaned over the chair and put her cheek next to Balthazar's. "What's your next move?" she whispered.

"Excuse me. Some space, please?"

"Hmm. Seems like he's got you beat." She winked at Vlad.

"What would you do then, miss chess master?" Balthazar scooted over so she had access to the whole board. Lenore didn't ponder long before moving his rook.

Zar scoffed so hard he spit. "Rooks cannot move diagonally! Sire, this woman..."

Lenore silently mocked his irate friend, and when she squished her face against Zar's, Vlad broke out into a full belly laugh.

Zar wiggled out from her grip and flew across the room with Lenore hot on his heels. Her mirth warmed the room more than the fire in the hearth as she chased him around the Hall.

Once she stopped to catch her breath, Vlad realized he hadn't properly greeted her. He rose and gently lifted her hand, placing a soft kiss on her knuckles. "Good morning, madam."

"Good morning, sir." Her silky voice made his heart beat faster.

"I prepared a dove for your breakfast. I hope my cooking is better than last time."

"I think anything would be better than that potato monstrosity you served her," Balthazar said from across the room.

"Hey now, it wasn't that bad. Was it?"

Lenore chuckled. "It wasn't the worst thing I've ever had, but it definitely wasn't the best."

They all laughed.

"Balthazar graciously agreed to share his berries with you," Vlad said.

"Did he now? Somehow, I find that hard to believe."

Zar stretched out a wing. "As long as you don't eat all my raspberries. Those are my favorite."

Vlad hurried into the kitchen and returned with breakfast. While Lenore ate, the men returned to their chess game.

"The sun has been out long enough to melt most of the snow on the road so the delivery boy should be here tomorrow afternoon," Vlad said.

Lenore swung her legs leisurely over the arm of the chaise and picked through the berries. "Excellent."

When Balthazar snatched up one of his knights, Vlad cursed.

"What language is that?" she asked. "You said it last night, too. I thought I may have dreamt it, but I recognize it."

He thought she'd been asleep when he whispered 'goodnight, my angel savior'.

"It's the lost language of my people. An older version of what many speak today."

"It's beautiful," she said.

*Yes, you are*, he thought.

Zar cleared his throat.

*Had he said that out loud?*

Lenore slunk deeper into the chair, but he caught her grinning. When she was through with breakfast, she insisted on cleaning her dishes, much to Vlad's protest.

They went to check on Marty, and while standing outside the barn, Vlad watched Balthazar make his way east on his typical post-breakfast flight. A single dark dot in the cloudy sky. He found his thoughts going to the loneliness that had plagued him all these years.

Was Zar lonely too?

Lenore led Marty out of the barn. "Everything all right?"

"Just wondering about Zar. He's been without his own kind like I have and I feel selfish for not wondering more often if he's lonely."

She tossed a blanket on Marty's back and threw the reins over his head. "He doesn't hang around other bats?" Lenore grabbed a fistful of the mule's mane and prepared to swing up on him, but Vlad gripped her by the waist and set her on top of the blanket.

"Thanks for the lift. You made that look so effortless."

He stood at her hip, head nearly level with her shoulder. He helped right Lenore's dress and adjusted the blanket beneath her. The air was warmer today but still required gloves and coats.

"Ready?" he asked.

"On your lead, Mr. Dracula."

He hadn't been called by his family name since he was a boy. As a man, Vlad wasn't sure how to feel about being the last of the Draculas. He had no way to make a name for himself. No legacy to leave in his separation from society.

Did the Dracula name mean anything at all anymore?

He walked beside Marty and guided them to the river where Lenore told him she'd killed the deer. He'd been impressed by her skill and apologized profusely she had to see him in bloodlust. He vowed to her, and himself, to never get close to that point ever again.

When they made it to the river, Lenore tied her mule to a tree with a long lead so he could graze. Half of the snowy area had melted, revealing thick grass Marty was happy to snatch up.

She sat next to him on a fallen log and looped her arm through his.

"I'll clear out one of the pastures when we get back so we don't have to come all the way down here for him to graze," he said.

"A whole pasture? That will take forever."

"You forget I am quite fast."

She nudged his arm, egging him on. "How fast?"

Vlad blurred as he made it to the ridge, then the river, then back up the mountain the way they'd come before returning to her side. His speed blew back her hair as he reappeared on the log.

"How do you do that?" she asked in a voice bursting with excitement. "It's amazing."

"I just have to imagine moving and my body does the rest," he said. "A product of one of the witch's many experiments."

His pulse quickened as panic rumbled under the surface at the mention of his tormentor.

*No, no, no. Please, not now.*

He tried to remember Lenore's words of help, taking deep breaths in and out, fighting to keep the tunnel vision from closing in on him.

*You're not in the hut anymore. You're here. You're safe.*

Lenore placed her hand on his. Lovely, concerned eyes peered up at him. "We don't have to talk about it."

Vlad took more steadying breaths. He despised not being able to master himself. To feel chained to the past so it affected his present. "I want to tell you. I just…"

As he worked on his breathing, Vlad focused on what brought him peace. The safety of the castle. His friendship with Balthazar. Lenore's kindness. The babbling river and the familiar smell of balsam in the crisp winter air. Out in the calm of nature, he began to come back to himself.

Lenore held his hand until his pulse returned to its slow beat. The tunnel vision never came, and the hot, prickling of his skin receded before it took hold of his whole body. "

"Wow. I've never been able to come down from those moments that quickly. Thank you for teaching me how to work it through it."

She rested her head on his arm and sidled up next to him. "Of course. I'm glad I could help."

When he felt it was emotionally safe to do so, Vlad told her his story. "The witch never told me her name, and she rarely told me what she was doing when she used her filthy magic on me. Eventually, I stopped asking."

Lenore began rubbing his forearm, still holding his hand.

Vlad took another deep breath. *He could do this.* The witch would not continue to ruin his life.

"Those welts you felt on my back are reactions to all the needles she stuck in me. Potion stations lined the hut where she held me captive and liquids of every color were injected into my body. Some made me feel like I was on fire. Some nearly froze my blood. Others, I felt nothing. Then I'd vomit minutes later.

"That's terrible!"

"Yes. It was," he said solemnly.

"What was her goal? To experiment just because she was a fucked up old witch?" Lenore flashed him an apologetic look. "Sorry for cursing. Balthazar was right. I do have a commoner's tongue."

He chuckled. "Don't apologize. I find your vernacular entertaining."

She went back to affectionately rubbing his arm, urging him to continue.

"The witch's goal was to create a superhuman, essentially. She'd tried on herself, which was how she became to look like she did. She told me one of her spells aged her thirty years in a single day and she was afraid of damaging herself further, so she sought someone else to continue her scientific horrors on.

"She wanted to give me superior eyesight and hearing. She succeeded partly in the hearing, but my eyes are more sensitive to light. On a bright day, I can't last more than a minute outside. Even on overcast days, I can't be out for too long before I get blinding headaches. It's why I do my feeding at night."

"Is that why the curtains in the Great Hall are always half drawn?"

He nodded. "The witch failed with my eyesight, but she succeeded in her most revolting of ideas. Making me need blood to survive."

"Does it taste…good?" Lenore asked.

"I wish it didn't, but it does. I don't even miss human food anymore."

*What pie was his favorite? Did he like salty foods as much as he remembered?* More questions he'd never find answers to.

"The strangest thing she achieved was my aging. In a week, I went from being fourteen to around twenty. The humans saw me when I was a bloodthirsty teenager during the one time I managed to escape before being caught again. I aged another five years or so after that, then stopped. I've looked roughly the same for over one-hundred years."

"What did she hope to achieve by doing that?"

Vlad swallowed. "Immortality."

Lenore's brows drew together. "So you're going to live forever?"

He shrugged. "I don't know. It's the number one question I have, and no one will ever be able to answer it for me."

"Surely someone has seen something like this before. Someone must have studied it. Maybe they could reverse it for you."

"I appreciate your enthusiasm, but you're the first person who's bothered to get to know me. People are afraid of what I am, and I doubt anyone would listen long enough to what I have to say."

Lenore perked up. "Maybe I could help make them see you aren't mean and scary. I could go to Shademoss and advocate for you. Help the townspeople see who you are at your core."

The optimism in her bright voice brought forth a dangerous emotion he'd cut out years ago. Hope. Hope for society to accept him.

"You would do that for me?" he asked.

She squeezed his arm. "You deserve the opportunity to get answers and to show people they don't need to fear you. I certainly don't."

He tucked a strand of hair behind her ear and trailed his fingertips along her cheek. "You truly are my angel savior." He repeated the last three words again in the old language, watching a smile of recognition burst across her face.

Vlad pressed his lips to hers. She let him control the pace, and when his panic never came, he smiled against her mouth.

God, this felt good. Felt right. Desperate to continue but not wanting to push his luck, Vlad kissed her forehead and smiled with glee.

They sat in silence, fingers interlocked, watching the river flow leisurely around the snow-capped stones.

*What if she did convince the people of Shademoss to accept him? What if he could have a real life around people and not have to be sequestered in the castle?*

The hope Vlad had exorcised flickered in his soul. A shred of it still remaining, brought back to life by the woman resting her head on his shoulder and holding his hand.

Never had such peace befallen him.

# 18

## BALTHAZAR

Balthazar skimmed the treetops, riding the wind. He rarely ventured this far from the castle, but the girl's presence these past few days uncovered old wants.

Watching the count come alive around Lenore drudged up feelings of hope that pushed Balthazar faster. He banked left and coasted around the sharp slope of the mountain. Split Peak—a bald cliff face tucked deep in the mountain side and perpetually in shadow—was just up ahead.

He descended on a cluster of pines a short distance from the cave and dropped into the thick of them. After careful maneuvering, Balthazar shrugged out of his collar and looked around for a properly suited branch. He hopped up the tree until he found one, hung up his collar, and used his foot to fluff out the fur around his neck the garment had matted. He didn't need to stand out any more than he already did.

The sprawling cave mouth split the mountain in a long vertical line with loud chittering coming from inside. The smell of guano carried on the breeze, stirring up a biological part of him that recognized it as the scent of home.

He'd sat outside the cave before, watching as he did now, but hadn't gone in. Discouraged, he'd left and happened to stumble upon a small family of bats, but they flew away as soon as he tried to talk to them, and he returned the castle defeated.

"Come on," he gritted out. "You can do this." After a few deep breaths and a big puff of his chest, Balthazar pushed off the branch.

His heart pounded as he entered the cave. The sounds were near deafening and the expanse of the cave left him in awe. There must have been thousands of bats in here. Balthazar couldn't help but smile as he flew deeper into the darkness, surveying the surroundings as his nocturnal vision heightened.

He wound around the stalactites and checked out the area. Everyone was busy sleeping, grooming themselves, or mulling about the cave that his existence went unnoticed. He was just another bat amongst a sea of many.

One of them.

He may love his life at the castle, but this place felt familiar in a way Vlad would never be able to understand. Though the count was his family now, it couldn't hurt to try and make friends with his own kind. It'd been a long time since he'd tried.

A few bats sat on an outcropping away from the others. *Best to start small*. Balthazar landed nearby and two of them looked up, but they went right back to drinking from the small pools in the rock. He followed their lead and did the same.

Since none of them protested his decision to join, Balthazar began grooming himself to look busy. He waited a while until he felt like he blended in and the nerves subsided, but before he could make the first move, a young bat approached him. Its eyes were large on its tiny face and it squeaked a greeting.

Balthazar squeaked back, trying to match the youngster's tones.

The little bat cocked its head and squeaked again.

He tried his best to remember how he used to communicate. He made sounds he thought meant, "Hello. I am a friend."

The little bat bristled and backed away.

Balthazar tried again, but it didn't work. He panicked and switched to words. "No! It's okay! I'm just trying to introduce myself."

The youngster started squealing wildly. The other bats rushed over and formed a circle, protecting the child. Squeaks and chitters came at him from all sides as the adults forced Zar back.

He retreated, chittering an apology, which only seemed to make them angrier.

"I..." Zar knew speaking in human words wouldn't work, but he couldn't decipher what they were saying. There were too many of them squawking in his face.

One of the bats snapped in his face and Zar jumped back. He slipped and tumbled down a craggy rock, splashing into a cold puddle and landing hard on something sharp. Wincing, Zar looked up to see the group watching over the ledge, still shouting at him. The cave grew louder as others nearby grew wise to what was happening.

Tears burned behind his eyes. He had to get out of here.

Zar hurriedly shook off the water and took flight. It wasn't long before more bats began chasing him toward the exit. He flew faster, eyes blurring, teeth nipping at his heels, his wings.

He whimpered.

Light shined up ahead. He was almost there.

Someone blindsided him and Balthazar slammed into the wall, hitting his head. Air whooshed out of him on impact and rattled his skull. Wheezing and disoriented, Zar blinked rapidly, head pounding.

He'd slid down the wall right into a grouping of bats who squealed at his abrupt arrival.

The others chasing him descended from above, and he narrowly avoided being knocked about again. Zar made for the exit, flapping harder, flying faster.

He zoomed around the stalactites to avoid the mob on his tail, and by the time he hit the open air, tears leaked from the corners of his eyes, merging with the rest of his soaked fur.

The squawking died down the further away he flew, finally free of their torment. When he made it back to the tree where he'd left his collar, Balthazar shimmied into the garment and left with haste.

He sniffled and let the wind take his tears as he made his way back to the river. He'd just wanted to try again. He expected some hesitation, but never...that. Their disapproving sounds echoed in his ears, and though he was long past the cave and moving at top speed, he couldn't outfly the hurt.

Balthazar flew so fast he overshot the humans, catching a glimpse of gold hair at the last second. He used the time it took to reroute to cage his emotions so neither of them would see his embarrassment. He landed on a branch nearby and immediately set to cleaning his wing to avoid looking at them.

"Why so far away, Zar?" The count had one arm slung around the girl and a deliriously happy grin on his face.

Zar's throat closed up. He wanted to be that happy. He forced himself to say, "Just tidying up, sire."

"Worried you don't look pretty enough?" Lenore said.

"I'm only trying to keep up with you, miss. Snow fell off a branch and soaked me. I must maintain my appearance." The polish in his faked words would surely hide the pain.

He caught Lenore's gaze and her smile paused as she noted his wet fur. She gave him a strange look like she could straight through his lie.

Vlad stood and offered her his hand. "Well, shall we all head back to the castle now?"

While the girl retrieved her mule, Balthazar tried his hardest to keep the tears at bay, but he couldn't stop thinking about how vicious the bats had been. How quickly they'd casted him out for being different.

Zar landed on the count's shoulder, shielding his face from them both. "I think I shall catch a ride and save my energy," he said in upbeat falsity. "Far better to reap the benefits of your labor, sire."

Vlad chuckled. "You're always welcome here."

His heart pinched. Forever welcome in one home. Barred from the other.

The humans chatted on the way home, and when they got lost in their conversation, Balthazar found his mind wandering as he stared at nothing in particular.

*Would he ever know a love like the one blossoming between Vlad and Lenore? Would he ever find a family amongst his own kind?*

When they arrived at the castle, Balthazar excused himself, saying he would see them later for dinner.

He hung up his collar on the coat rack in his room and prepared for sleep. Balthazar hung upside down on the dowel stretching across the room Vlad had constructed and wrapped his wings around his body. Under the cover of his self-made darkness, he wished to never relive such a horrible experience again.

He could rely on the home he'd made here, and that would have to be enough.

Something bright flashed across his eyelids, waking him.

A candelabra illuminated a pale face peeking through the crack in the door. "May I come in?" Lenore asked.

Zar kept his wings tight around him. He was still so tired. "Is something the matter?"

## VLAD AND FRIENDS

The girl let herself in, shut the door, and set the candelabra on the side table. She made herself at home and plopped in the padded rocking chair. "I came to ask you the same question."

"I'm fine."

She rubbed her arms. "It's freezing in here." Lenore grabbed a blanket from the pile in the bassinet that'd been left untouched since he'd claimed the nursery as his bedroom. "So, what's wrong?"

"Nothing. Just getting my beauty sleep before dinner."

She cocked her head. "You were quiet on the ride here. Not your usual, sassy self."

"I was tired."

She looked around the nursery. "Was this Vlad's room when he was a baby?"

"I...I don't actually know."

"All this time together and you never asked?"

"We may be old friends, but the count's lodgings as an infant never came up."

She chuckled despite his curt reply. "That's because men don't talk enough to one another."

"We talk plenty."

Lenore began rocking in the chair with a knowing look on her face.

He sighed and righted himself, perching on top of the dowel like a bird. Another thing that set him apart from other bats. Different anatomy. Different speech. Just more damning differences that would make it so he never belonged.

"What is it you want, Lenore?"

"I want you to tell me what's wrong. You left bright and cheery. Well, as cheery as you can be, and returned...different."

"I told you, I'm just tired."

"Vlad may have believed that, but I don't. So why don't you tell me what's bothering you?"

"Everything's fine."

She stopped rocking. "You men may not talk, but I know you're upset and I want to help."

He blew out a frustrated breath. Apparently, her stubbornness applied to someone other than herself. "It's nothing you can help me with."

"Try me." The challenge in her smile finally tore down the walls of his ire.

"You're not going to leave until I tell you, are you?"

She shook her head.

"Fine." Balthazar told her what happened, eyes glued to the floor to avoid the disgrace. When he was finished, he looked up to see her smile gone and the rocking chair still.

"Don't look at me with that pity. It's embarrassing enough as it is," he said.

Her eyes were glossy marbles in the candlelight. "I'm so sorry, Balthazar."

The longer he looked at Lenore, the more her eyes watered. Soon, his were doing the same. He'd expected her to tell him to get over it or ridicule him for the foolish attempt, but she didn't.

Lenore patted the blanket wrapped around her. "Come sit."

Normally, he would have told her he was no lap dog, but his defenses were down. Her pleading eyes had him fluttering over and landing in a nest-like cushion she'd made in the blanket.

"You can lay down."

Reluctantly, he did. Balthazar lied on his side, facing away from her as she began rocking. "What now?" he asked.

She ran her hand along his fur.

His head shot up, stern eyes meeting hers. Perhaps his defenses weren't *all* the way down. "I do not need to be pet like a dog."

"Vlad doesn't pet you?"

He scoffed. "Men do not pet one another."

A slow smile grew on her face before she started laughing, eventually making Balthazar do the same. The sentence sounded ridiculous.

He laid back down, facing the window.

Lenore ran her hand from the top of his head down his side in slow strokes.

*Damn his pride.* It felt phenomenal.

Occasionally, she would scratch the thicker fur around his neck where his collar normally sat. Her nails felt so good, and after a long time sitting in companionable silence, the kind gesture finally pulled the truth out of him.

"They were so mean," he whispered.

Her motions paused, but only for a moment.

His voice cracked. "Am I really so different that they couldn't accept me?"

"Sometimes others are just afraid of what they don't understand, but that doesn't mean they can't come around. It might just take time."

Balthazar squeaked his sorrow as tears fell and wet the blanket under his cheek. He lost the ability to speak and Lenore seemed to understand he just needed someone to be there. No words. No solutions. Just a comforting presence to show him he wasn't alone.

He would have thanked her for it, but the tender, reassuring movements of her hand stroking his fur, the warm cradle of the blanket, and rock of the chair lulled him into a peaceful sleep where the memories of the cave couldn't find him.

# 19

## VLAD

Vlad peeked his head into Balthazar's room. The bat snored, but he wasn't hanging from his dowel like usual. Vlad stepped inside and spotted him curled in the blanket on Lenore's lap. She was fast asleep in the rocking chair, head lolled to the side.

A smile burst across his face seeing the two cuddled up together, but upon closer inspection, he noticed a dark spot on the blanket under Balthazar's cheek.

Had Zar been crying?

Lenore mentioned she thought something was wrong with him on the ride back from the river, but Vlad hadn't been so sure. Seeing his friend now, he hated knowing Zar was hurting and that he'd dismissed it.

Vlad set the bowl of berries he'd brought on the windowsill before gently nudging his friend. "Zar," he whispered.

Balthazar snorted, eyes rolling forward.

"I brought you dinner," he said softly, pointing at the berries.

"Time for dinner already?" The fur around his eyes was damp, tugging at the count's heartstrings.

"Are you all right?" Vlad asked.

"Better now." He glanced at Lenore, and the appreciative look told Vlad everything he needed to know. "Don't let her go, sire."

"I don't plan to."

"Good." Zar flew to the windowsill and began picking through the bowl. "Because that woman is good for both of us."

Vlad stared at her adoringly. "She certainly is." He gently scooped her up, careful not to wake her. When they were out in the hall, Lenore jerked awake.

"Oh, it's just you," she said, beaming up at him.

He set her on her feet. "Just me."

"Did I fall asleep in Zar's room?"

"You were out cold so I planned to take you to your room. Unless you're ready for dinner."

She looked around the hall and her eyes landed on his door. "You told me this was your room but I never got to see it on our tour."

He didn't miss the unasked question. "Would you like to see it?"

Her doe eyes narrowed. "I'd love to."

Vlad's throat instantly went dry.

Lenore swished her hips as she entered his bedroom, glancing at him over her shoulder.

Realizing he'd forgotten to tidy up, Vlad buzzed about the room at his vampiric speed, picking up the dress shirts and socks scattered about.

Lenore snickered. "Too late. I already saw that the prim and proper royal was secretly messy."

The fact his speed no longer alarmed her was a luxury Vlad didn't know how much he needed. He could be himself around her. Lenore had seen him in bloodlust and in the revealing of his superhuman abilities. She had seen it all, and she was still here. Stranding in his room with a longing in her eyes that said, 'come and get me'.

The air between them thrummed with desire. Heartbeats quickening from an aching need to be close to one another. To feel skin on skin, breaths mingling, and hands roaming. Another unasked question he wanted to answer.

Vlad walked toward her with purpose. She'd healed a part of him that had been broken for so long and now nothing would keep him from having her.

Her lips parted as he approached, chest heaving.

Their lips joining fiercely as Vlad embraced her. Her warmth was an immediate comfort and the feel of her against him was something he'd never tire of.

"Vlad." Her plea came out of soft. Desperate. Stirring a feeling in his chest. And...*lower*.

He walked her backward, hands full of her voluptuous body. When they made it to the edge of his massive four-post bed, he spun her around tugged on the dress ribbons, whispering in her ear, "May I?"

"Yes," Lenore said, breathless.

He worked her lavender strings and slid her sleeves down, kissing the top of her bare shoulder. His cock strained against his pants, and he pulled Lenore closer, letting her feel how much he wanted her.

She tipped her head back, eyes closed as silky golden hair brushed his neck. Though the pulse in her throat thrummed, he had no desire for human blood and would never do anything to hurt her. A soft press of his lips against the column of her throat was a silent promise that he would be nothing but gentle.

Vlad slid the dress off her body and let it pool at her feet. The satin chemise she wore underneath folded loosely around her waist and strained around her hips, taunting him. He couldn't keep his hands off her. She was a decadent dessert he wanted to take his time savoring. He kissed her neck while his hands discovered her shapely form.

Lenore reached behind her, sliding a hand into his hair. Her soft moans and rapid breaths drove him wild.

He needed her. Now. Vlad began removing his jacket.

She whirled, and the sight of her nipples against the satin had him moving faster. He yanked off his bowtie and threw it aside, feverishly working the buttons on his vest.

Lenore helped tear at his clothing until he was left standing in only his undershorts. Calloused fingers trailed down his chest. "Are you sure you're ready to do this?" she asked.

The panic remained quiet. It would not ruin this moment for him. Vlad gripped her chin and placed a soft kiss on her lips. "More than ready." Embarrassment at his inexperience tried to work its way in, but he wouldn't let it. Not with her. "You'll have to show me how to do it though."

Her answering smile was everything he'd been missing.

"We'll go at your pace," Lenore said, trailing a nail along his smooth jaw. She nipped at his bottom lip.

"I'd do that back but I don't want to get you with my fangs." If he ever spilled a drop of her blood, Vlad knew he'd never forgive himself.

"Please, don't," she chuckled. Lenore gripped his waistband and began pushing his undershorts down his hips. Vlad let her, and when his cock sprang free, she gasped.

"Oh my."

He looked down at himself. "What? What's wrong?"

She slid a finger along the length of him, making him twitch in pleasure. Her eyes dragged up to meet his. "Absolutely nothing is wrong. I should have expected a large cock on a man of your height but you are more impressive than I realized."

His body ignited when she gripped his cock and began working him the way he did sometimes when he was alone.

"God, it feels so much better when you do it," he groaned.

Lenore kissed his chest, tugging on him slowly.

With eyes tightly shut, Vlad let himself relax in her grip. He never wanted her to stop. When she did, he practically begged her to continue.

Lenore stepped back with a sultry grin and shimmied out of her chemise completely, taking the rest of her undergarments with it. Silky hair fell behind one shoulder and loose waves framed her left breast. She stood completely naked, and Vlad could have sworn she glowed. Truly the angel savior he called her.

He'd never seen a naked woman in person, only in the art books in his father's study, but the images held nothing on her.

"You are the most beautiful thing I have ever seen," Vlad said in utter awe. "A goddess."

She took his hand and led him to the bed. Lenore laid on her back and positioned Vlad over top her. With their height difference, he had to hunch slightly to kiss her, but Vlad didn't care. He would do anything to keep chasing this euphoric feeling rushing through him.

What was it? Desire? Passion? Lust?

Her soft body arching beneath him had their kisses turning needier. They rocked slowly against one other, and Vlad didn't flinch when she moved her hands to his back, brushing his welts.

When the horrible memories didn't flood his mind, he rejoiced. They began moving in a rhythmic motion and he didn't know how it could get any better than this.

"Vlad."

His name on her shuttering breath made his cock pulse. He pushed a strand of hair back from her flushed cheek. "Yes?"

"Do you want to have sex?"

*Weren't they already doing that?* "I, uhh...thought we..."

"You'll put this inside me." She reached down between them and repositioned his cock further down so the tip rested against something wet and warm.

"Feel that?"

He nodded, anticipation growing.

"That's what happens when a woman is excited to be with you. It means you've gotten her aroused."

Vlad had heard that word between giggling servants but he hadn't known what it meant.

"The tip of your cock is wet because you're aroused too." She didn't speak to him in a condescending way, knowing he'd never been with anyone. Lenore was patient and understanding, and he adored her all the more for it.

"Are you sure you're ready? Sure you want this?"

"Yes," he said quickly. "More than anything."

She beamed. "Just go slow so you don't accidentally hurt me."

He made minute movements, feeling her open for him as he pressed his cock against the wet place on her lower body. He went inside her a little further and she gasped, hands squeezing his hips.

He stilled. "Are you okay?"

She encouraged him by tugging on his hips. "Yes. You're just large. But, God, you feel so good, Vlad."

Male dominance swelled up inside him at the compliment. He pushed in a little further until all of him was inside her.

"Oh, wow." He had never felt anything so wonderful.

Lenore kissed him, and the natural urge to move had him rocking into her. She gripped his hips and helped guide his motions. "Just like that. Keep that pace for now."

His cock slid in and out of her as moans of pleasure came from them both.

Vlad had never been a religious man, but he called out to God regardless. "God-damn, this feels good."

Lenore chuckled. "That may be the first time I've ever heard you curse."

He deepened their kisses, beginning to move faster. Excitement rushed through him like a roaring river at being pressed against her breasts, looking down at her beautiful face as a growing urge hardened his cock even more.

Vlad knew enough about sex to know it could get a woman pregnant, but he wasn't quite sure how.

As if reading his mind, Lenore said a bit breathlessly, "When you feel like you're about to reach your pinnacle, make sure you ease out of me. You can spill yourself right here." She pointed to her belly.

"On you?" *That didn't seem polite.*

She moaned, head falling back against the pillow. "Yes. Yes, it's okay."

Vlad wanted to soak in the moment but the pressure inside him was rapidly rising. He gripped one of her supple thighs, fingers pressing into her heated skin as Lenore encouraged him faster. The feel of her body melding with his, their mingling breaths, the view this position gave him, had Vlad erupting.

He pulled out and grunted his absolute euphoria into her neck as he spilled onto her stomach. Lenore clung to his back, squeezing him with her legs and moaning.

Vlad was overcome after he'd finished, feeling light-headed and in such a glorious daze that he couldn't stop smiling. "That was amazing. Did you feel it too? The orgasm, I mean?"

She smiled softly, touching his cheek. "It's a bit harder for women to reach that point."

His face dropped.

"Don't worry," she reassured him, pushing the hair back from his face. "It felt wonderful for me too. Just sometimes, different things have to happen for me to get to the point you just did."

He was suddenly aware that they were talking while she was covered in his mess.

Vlad quickly rolled off her. "Let me get something to clean you off with." Her body was slick where his cock had been, so he thought she might like a warm towel.

In his spacious washroom, Vlad ran a hand towel under the faucet until the water warmed. He rung it out and hurried back into the bedroom. "Will this work to clean you?"

Lenore pushed up onto her elbows and nodded. Between her legs seemed like the best place to start.

"Ohh," she said when he pressed the cloth to her. "I didn't expect it to be warm. It feels nice. Soothing."

"Taking care of you is the least I could do after what you did for me." When he was through, Vlad began wiping his mess off her stomach.

"Well, you've already done more for me post-sex than any man ever has, so it's you that deserves the praise."

She was a part of a thriving world and had been for years. Of course he'd expected her to have had sex before, but hearing her say it sent a pang of jealousy through him. He finished cleaning her in silence and disposed of the cloth in the waste basket.

"Is something wrong?" Lenore asked when he came back into the room.

"I'm just having a hard time picturing you doing that with another man." He ran a hand through his hair. "It makes me—"

"Jealous?" The taunting smile she wore had him stalking forward.

Lenore squeezed her legs together as he approached and started giggling. "Vlad Dracula, are you jealous of meager village men?"

He crawled over her and wrapped her legs back around him. "Yes."

She snickered. "Don't be. What you and I just shared was more meaningful than any time I've ever had. Truly."

His jealousy eased but doubt crept its way in. "You're not just saying that because you pity me?"

Her brows furrowed, smiled fading.

Vlad moved to a sitting position and covered his lower half with the sheets, Lenore following suit.

He sighed. "I'm sorry." He knew it was just his insecurities coming out.

"Hey." Lenore turned his head to look at her. "I know this is all new to you and these feelings are normal. I don't pity you for feeling them. If anything, I'm angry."

"Did I make you angry?" He hadn't wanted to do that at all.

She put her hand on his. "I'm not angry with *you*. I'm angry with your parents for not protecting you. I'm angry they let the witch take their son and even angrier for everything she did to you. I'm angry other people robbed you of the experiences of growing up. Of learning, and exploring, and discovering life. None of that should have happened to you, Vlad."

She squeezed his hand. "I care deeply for you. You are the kindest man I've ever known, and you deserve all the time you need to navigate all aspects of life. I'm merely grateful you're allowing me to be a part of it."

He would never be able to put the happiness occurring in his heart into words, no matter how many times he'd put ink to paper. The encouragement and kindness this woman radiated had altered him forever.

"You have turned my world upside down, Lenore. And for that, I thank you. I was simply jealous others have gotten to know your light and that I'm only sharing in it."

She sidled up into the crook of the arm he draped around her. Vlad brushed a thumb across her bottom lip. "I just want you all to myself, but I know that's selfish."

She smirked. "Yes, it is. But be selfish and keep me as long as you want."

His eyes widened. "You mean—"

"I want to stay with you. Shademoss can wait a while longer."

She wanted to stay. She wanted *him*. Lenore squealed as he tackled her to the bed.

It wasn't long before he was back inside her, the two of them sharing hot breath as want and desire transformed into something he'd only read about in books. Something akin to how he imagined love must feel like.

# 20

# Vlad

He awoke with Lenore's hair spilling across his arm, tickling him.

*I want to stay with you*, she'd said last night.

Overwhelmed with gratitude, Vlad buried himself inside her, chasing another orgasm and helping Lenore to find hers. Twice.

He may have nearly a century and a half of knowledge from the many books in his library, but he learned more last night than he had in his entire existence. Lenore taught him how to please her and showed him different positions he was more than happy to try out.

The inky night bled into dawn by the time they'd exhausted themselves. He'd asked to go again, surprised at his stamina, but she could hardly hold her eyes open.

"We have many more days," she said before falling asleep in his arms.

He held her close as the morning sun did its best to pierce the heavy drapes in his room. Vlad hadn't slept in this late since...ever. He would have lingered in his cocoon of happiness, but the delivery boy would be arriving soon with the provisions he'd ordered and he still needed to repair the axle on her cart.

Lenore stirred. Heavy-lidded eyes and a sleepy smile greeted him. "Good morning, handsome."

He kissed her. "Good morning, my angel."

After lying there reminiscing on their nightly activities and discussing breakfast, Lenore went to her room to bathe while Vlad did the same.

He finished dressing and fixed the lapels to his jacket, smoothing back his hair and smiling at the rumpled mess of a bed.

Before she came down for breakfast, he retrieved her cart and brought it back to the castle. The axle wouldn't be too difficult to repair, and he found the tools he thought would prove helpful in the tack room of the barn. Marty whinnied a greeting from the pasture Vlad had cleared out, content to stuff himself on the grass that was now only patched in snow.

After he fed and prepared breakfast for Lenore, Vlad stood at the window in the Great Hall overlooking the garden, watching Balthazar gather berries from the vine and place them in a basket.

With the sun shining brightly, Vlad donned his top hat, squinting until he made it out to the shaded terrace. "Nice day," he said to Zar by way of greeting.

Zar took the wicker handle in his mouth and hefted it over to the terrace, setting it on the table. "It is, isn't it?"

Birds chirped, and a mourning dove cooed from atop a spire as the forest thawed. An unusual warmth for this time of year, but he was glad. It would make the delivery's boy's journey easier.

# VLAD AND FRIENDS

"Quite a lot of food you have there," Vlad said. "Worked up an appetite?"

Balthazar chomped on a blackberry. "They're also for Lenore. If anyone worked up an appetite last night, it was her." Zar flashed him a devilish grin.

Vlad blushed. "I don't know what you're talking about."

The two chuckled.

"I'm happy for you, sire. Truly."

"Thank you, friend. You know, she asked to stay here with us for a while."

Zar licked fruit juices off his lips. "How wonderful! Though she'll need to work on keeping it down. Had a hard time sleeping last night because of that woman's sounds."

Lenore came around the corner.

"Speaking of squealers..."

"Balthazar!" Vlad whisper-yelled.

The bat snickered.

"How are my two handsome men this morning?" Lenore squished her face so hard against Zar's that his cheeks deflated and berries spilled out of his mouth.

"My breakfast, woman! I was going to share with you, but now..."

She swiped a raspberry as Zar swatted her with his wing. "Diabolical thief!"

Vlad laughed harder when Lenore patted Zar's head and he tucked himself into a tight, angry little ball.

"May I bite her, sire?"

"No, you may not."

"Hmph." Balthazar shielded his basket. "If she stays, we're going to have to figure out berry rations."

Lenore snuck around and snagged another berry, laughing at the bat's outrage. She surveyed the garden with a hand at her brow. "This is a great space for food, but what about flowers? Something pretty to use as a border."

"I hadn't thought of that," Vlad said. "Some color would look nice."

"Could I plant some?"

He could deny her nothing. "Anything you want."

"I am partial to peonies," Zar said with a full mouth.

"Maybe you could ask your delivery boy to bring seeds next time."

Vlad beamed at how she spoke of the future. A future that included him.

Her voice hiked up. "Or maybe I could go to Shademoss and buy some myself! See the town. Stroll the market." Lenore twirled and her dress fanned out around her. "I could use the opportunity to talk to the people there about you! Let them know they have nothing to fear."

The shine in her bright eyes made it impossible for Vlad not to admire her, but what she was saying made his chest tighten.

*What if the townspeople didn't believe what she said about him? Or worse, what if she loved Shademoss and never came back?*

The thought crossed his mind when she first mentioned it, but not wanting to be selfish, he said, "Maybe you could speak to the boy when he arrives. He usually puts my items in the box by the back gate where I leave the money, then I retrieve them once he's gone. You could show him you're safe here."

"I can definitely do that."

"And do try to watch your language," Balthazar added. "We want the boy and the rest of the town to know we are refined, learned people."

"But you're a bat."

Balthazar frowned. "You know what I mean."

"All right, I'll try my God-damned best." Lenore stuck up her nose, mimicking the bat.

As if on cue, the sound of the bell on the boy's cart jingled in the distance. "Come now, Zar. Let's leave her to it." Vlad grabbed the basket of berries and waited for Zar to hop on his shoulder. Lenore bounded toward the gate, the perfect portrait of color and life.

Inside the castle, Vlad watched from the window. Lenore stood at the edge of the estate in the sky-blue dress she'd worn the first day she'd come into his life. She was so bright. So out of place in his dark home and the monotonous colors of the mountain.

When the boy came up the road, he stopped his donkey short. Even from afar, Vlad could see the shock in his wide eyes.

Lenore approached him, gesturing and likely talking in that confident way of hers.

"What do you think she's saying?" Zar asked, still perched on his shoulder.

"Hopefully something that works out in our favor."

Not being able to hear their conversation had Vlad shifting on his feet.

"Everything all right, sire?"

He swallowed. "Lenore being at the castle has shown me just how isolated I've kept us. There is no society here. No way to experience a full life. She has big dreams, and if she stays, there isn't a way for them to come true. You saw her out in the garden. How excited she was to visit the town."

They were both quiet for a moment. Vlad wanted her to stay at the castle more than ever, but if he caged a wild horse, it wouldn't be long before she tried to jump the fence.

Balthazar seemed unsure what to say, which made Vlad even more certain he was right. Would Lenore be happy here? How long would she be satisfied with only the two of them for company without the society she longed to discover?

The answer he knew to be true made his stomach turn, so he changed the subject. "Where did you run off to the other day at the river?"

They stayed facing forward. Admissions were easier when eye contact wasn't involved.

"Lenore didn't tell you?"

Vlad shook his head.

"Hmm. Admirable of her." Zar took a minute to speak, and when he did, his words came out low. "I tried conversing with the bats in the cave at Split Peak. It didn't go well."

"Do you want to talk about it?"

"That's all right. She and I already did."

A smile curved Vlad's lips. "Well, I'm here for you too, friend."

The comfortable silence between them acted as Balthazar's confirmation. They had always been there for each other and always would, but Lenore had created a bridge, forcing the two to confront their emotions head on.

The boy unloaded the last crate and Lenore waved goodbye. When he was gone, the men ventured back outside.

She surveyed the delivery with both hands on her hips. "You, Vlad Dracula, need much help in the ways of provisions."

He looked at the crates. "Did I do something wrong?"

"Not wrong, exactly." She removed a few of the lids. "But the portions are all off. You don't need six sacks of sugar and only one bag of apples."

Zar stuck his tongue through a tear in one of the bags and jolted. "Oh, I like sugar! Six bags may not be enough."

She laughed and patted Vlad on the shoulder. "What would you boys do without me?"

As if he might lose her in that moment, Vlad wrapped her in a hug and kissed her repeatedly.

"Ugh, sire."

Lenore chuckled. "Do you want kisses too, Zar?"

The bat tried to fly away but she caught him and kissed his cheek repeatedly as he vehemently demanded to be let go.

Leaving the two to their daily torment, Vlad hauled the crates into the kitchen. When he was through, they were at the tail end of their silly argument. Balthazar got the last word before heading out for his morning flight.

The two of them unpacked the provisions in the kitchen, and he caught Lenore chewing on the inside of her cheek as she stared at a few items. He could tell she was deep in thought.

Vlad set one of the sugar sacks down. "Something on your mind?"

"What do you think about me going into town to buy a few things we're missing? This will only be enough for a few meals and I don't want you to have to hunt for me all the time. While I'm there, I could talk to the townspeople. Get an idea of how they view you and use that opportunity to tell them about my time here."

Lenore hopped on the counter and swung her legs. "I could take Marty and my cart, buy some feed and hay, a few more day dresses, and some more proportional rations. What do you think?"

He fidgeted with the string on the bag of sugar. "I don't mind hunting for you. You don't have to leave."

"I'll come back. I just want to make it easier on everyone and pick up a few things that don't require so much work to make."

Everything in him feared she would love the town and choose to stay. With much difficulty, he said, "You're welcome to get whatever you need. I have plenty of money. Though I do have concerns about the other part of your plan."

Lenore grabbed his hand and pulled him toward her. "Like what?"

He stood in between her legs, staring down at her. "I know what people think of me. That I'm a blood-thirsty monster. A demon sent straight from Hell. Their minds haven't been changed in over a century." Vlad brushed his knuckles down her cheek. "I doubt one person's word will be enough to convince them. Even yours."

"I can see why you'd be worried. The delivery boy thought you were forcing me to stay here." She chuckled, but there was a sadness to it. Lenore skimmed her fingers along his. "It will take time, and it may take multiple visits, but I know I can convince them. One day, they'll see what I see."

He searched her gaze for confirmation that she was right. That everything would go smoothly and he'd be welcomed into town, but the apprehension wouldn't leave.

"What if it doesn't work?" he said softly.

She cupped his cheek. Determined, jade eyes bored into his. "I will make it work. Because you deserve it."

He pushed aside his fear of the future and focused on Lenore instead. If anyone could convince them, it would be her. She was too enigmatic not to be listened to. Vlad kissed her, and soon, explorative fingers slipped under clothing and brushed skin.

"Zar will be gone for about an hour," he said. "We could..."

Lenore giggled. "We could."

He dropped to his knees and stuck his head under her dress.

"In here?"

Vlad gripped her thighs and spread them, grateful she'd taught him how to do this particular act. He slid a hand up her stomach and nudged her back until she was lying down.

The woman of his dreams gasped when he slid his tongue along the most sensitive part of her, and though there was food in the kitchen, Vlad devoured the only meal he really wanted.

# 21

## VLAD

Balthazar sat on Marty's rump, inspecting the mule's harness like it was the finest piece of craftsmanship he'd ever seen. "Genius," he muttered.

Hours earlier, Vlad fixed the axle and replaced a few nails in the siding while Lenore watched, nibbling on her bottom lip as he worked bare-chested in the barn. Though the weather had warmed, it was still cool enough for steam to rise from his muscled, sweaty body. He'd been more than happy for the job to be interrupted by Lenore's passionate kissing.

After she climbed into the seat of the cart, Vlad handed her the reins. "Promise you'll be careful?" He'd packed a basket full of more food than she could possibly need for the trip there and the ride back tomorrow morning.

She squeezed his hand. "I promise. And I'll be on my best behavior."

Balthazar snorted.

"I'll miss you too, Zar," she said.

He flapped into the seat next to her. "If you find any strawberries—"

"Yes, yes. And peaches."

Zar grinned. "Good. Don't forget."

She patted him on the head and he frowned, even though they all knew he liked it.

Vlad's face was drawn as he checked her cart again. "Just want to make sure everything's secure."

She let him fuss and tugged the wide brim hat he'd given her lower on her forehead. The sun beamed down on them and the snow sat in patches along the road. Hopefully travel would be easy.

"I wish I could go with you." Vlad hated the pitiful tone in his voice. He wanted to go in part to discover the town with her, but also to make sure she returned to him. He didn't care if it was an overzealous move, he would cling to the gift he'd been given for as long as he could.

Lenore leaned down and took his face in her hands. "I will come back straight after breakfast and see you well before sundown."

She kissed him, imprinting the feel of her soft lips to memory. Lips that had tasted her on the kitchen counter a couple hours ago, bringing his angel savior to a wondrous climax.

"Be good, Balthazar," she said.

The bat fluttered over to Vlad's shoulder. "I'm always good."

"I'll see you both tomorrow."

Balthazar squeaked, likely picturing peaches he could sink his little fangs into.

Vlad forced a grin.

Lenore snapped the reins and the mule begrudgingly started walking. She waved 'goodbye' as Balthazar flapped a wing and Vlad lifted a heavy hand in return.

When she'd almost made it out of view, Lenore turned in her seat.

The sight of her leaving gutted him. As she disappeared over the hill, the pit forming in his stomach tightened into a dull ache. Vlad thought he might be sick. "I must feed. I shall be back a while later."

*A worthy excuse.*

"As you wish, sire. I will be inside."

Vlad needed space to worry without causing his friend concern. He would go to the river, pace and fret until he could no longer stand it, then feed and return home, doing the same tomorrow. Anything to pass the time until his salvation returned.

The instant the sun dipped behind the trees the next day, Vlad's throat went tight. He stared at the road through the window in the Great Hall. "She's not here."

Balthazar sat on his pillow, their game of chess forgotten. "Perhaps she's just delayed or got a late start."

His stomach turned. "What if something happened? What if her cart broke down again? What if she's hurt?" The fire danced wildly in the hearth as if reacting to his concern.

"I'm sure she's fine, sire. Try not to worry. It's only just now sunset."

Vlad pulled himself away from the window and paced the length of the room. "No. Something's wrong. I just know it. She said she'd be here by sundown. She promised." He'd never heard his voice so shrill. So shaken. His palms began to sweat.

"Why don't we continue our game?"

Vlad chewed on his fingernails. He never did that.

"Sire."

*What if Lenore was attacked by bandits? What if animals got her?* His heartbeat was a thundering herd of horses against his sternum.

"She said she'd be here."

"Why don't I fly the path? See if I can spot her on the road."

Vlad stopped pacing. "Yes! Good idea, Zar." He hurried to the back gate. The road leading to Shademoss was dark and he wished desperately for a lantern to show, a squeaky wheel to sound, a snort from Marty. Something. Anything. But the night was quiet. Snow lingered in the woods but the roads were clear and it hadn't rained.

*Where in the devil was she?*

"I'll fly as fast as I can and report back as soon as possible."

Vlad chewed his cuticle until it bled. He hissed. "Thank you."

"She will be here soon, sire. I'm sure of it."

He watched Balthazar fly until he was completely out of sight. Vlad would have stayed and stared at the road until Lenore returned, but if those irritating people from Newthorn decided to show up again, he didn't want to be caught unaware in his worry.

Reluctantly, the count returned to the Great Hall and resumed pacing. He shrugged out of his jacket. Loosened his necktie. *Why was it so warm in here?*

Vlad tried to calm himself. "Deep breaths in and out. Just like Lenore taught you." After the third breath, his heart rate slowed. "It's okay. She just got delayed. She'll be here. Balthazar will find her."

Try as he might, Vlad couldn't convince himself that something terrible hadn't happened. He pressed his fingers to his temples, willing away the bad thoughts like he used to do in the witch's hut.

"It's okay. It's okay. It's okay. She's coming back."

A sickening idea struck him. *What if she wasn't coming back? What if...*

"No. No. She wouldn't do that." Vlad physically shook his head so the thought couldn't take root. He had to do something to distract himself. He'd already fed and made sure to fill a few extra emergency jars with blood while he was out, and since he couldn't stand around and wait outside, Vlad went to a place he hadn't been in a while.

As he made his way there, he took note of all the lit candles that had become his nightly ritual for Lenore. She had brightened the castle with her laughter and compassion. Brought life into his home. Taken him out of the darkness. A place he never wished to return.

If she didn't come back, how long would it take for the cobwebs to return and the gloom to seep back into everything?

Vlad entered a room on the fourth floor. The door creaked open, revealing his father's study. God, it smelled exactly like it used to. Leather-bound books, parchment, and smoke from his father's pipe.

A myriad of emotions rushed through him. Happiness from sitting on his father's knee as the man went over his ledgers. Contentment as Vlad slumbered with the family dog on the chaise in the corner while his father tended to correspondence. Sadness for missing the man and anger for the same.

He lit a few candles and took his time perusing the space. Dust coated the shelves, but the oak desk was preserved in its purpose. Ink pots and quills lined the compartments. One of the pots was missing its lid, the ink inside dry and cracked. Yellowed papers sat in stacks with dates long since passed.

Vlad opened the main drawer. His father's pipe sat on a cloth with blackened spots where the bowl rested. He gingerly picked it up, remembering being severely scolded for trying to smoke it once. It still felt forbidden to hold. He turned over the pipe of mahogany and ebony with a ring of pure gold curling around the stem.

For years, he'd admired his father for the man's steely resolve. His ability to effectively help run a country. The steadfast dedication to his people. Dedicated to everyone except his own son when it came down to it.

"Why wasn't I enough for you, father?" Vlad said to the pipe. Tears burned his eyes. "Why?" he gritted out.

He snapped the stem off and threw the pieces into the hearth, quickly lighting the logs and watching the pipe burn.

He didn't matter enough to his parents, and perhaps, he didn't matter enough to Lenore either and that's why she hadn't returned.

## VLAD AND FRIENDS

Not because she was hurt, but because she'd chosen to stay in Shademoss.

She had so much life in her that couldn't be contained to one place, and he knew deep down she would never be satisfied with a simple life with him. Vlad just hadn't wanted to let himself believe it.

In his castle, utterly alone for the first time ever, his inner resolve collapsed. He flung the papers off the desk. Ink pots rolled across the floor, pens scattered, and old notebooks fell open as they hit the ground.

Vlad slid to the floor, covering his face with his hands, sobbing.

Lenore had left him. For who could love a man so broken? Someone with crippling panic and nightmares and marred skin, who couldn't fit in with the rest of the world? Why would a beautiful woman with ambition ever want to stay with someone like him?

He couldn't blame her. He couldn't offer Lenore much other than his devotion, but he'd been devoted to his family and his kingdom, and that hadn't worked out either.

Vlad wasn't sure how long he sat there, tears frozen on his face as he stared at the fire when Balthazar entered the room.

"Sire?" his friend said softly.

Vlad slowly turned his head, knowing he would find Balthazar alone. The bat was soaking wet. Lightning flashed through the window.

He hadn't even heard the storm.

Zar's eyes went wide as soon as he met the count's empty stare. "Sire? Are you all right? Why are you on the floor?"

"Any sign of her?"

Balthazar shook out the water from his fur. "I flew a little further to make sure, but the path remained dark. I didn't see a cart or wheel marks on the road." He let out a defeated breath. "I'm sorry I couldn't find her. I-I don't know where she could be."

Vlad looked back at the fire. "She's gone, Zar."

The bat removed his dripping collar and set it by the fire to dry. "Maybe she decided to stay another night. Maybe she didn't get to talk to everyone she wanted to about you."

Everything inside Vlad had gone numb. His worst fear had happened again. He'd been abandoned.

"I knew she wanted to start a life there. I just thought I'd get to be a part of it. I thought *we* would get to be a part of it. I was stupid to believe that."

"She didn't leave us, sire. I refuse to believe that. I've seen how much she cares for you. I see the way her face lights up when she sees you."

A tear slid down Vlad's cheek. "I want to believe that, but we're vampires. Destined to be outcasts. Not to belong."

Zar's eyes fell to the floor.

Remembering his friend's encounter in the cave, Vlad immediately regretted his words. "I'm sorry. I didn't mean—"

"It's all right." Zar turned his attention to the fire, and Vlad did the same. They sat on the floor until the rain receded and the lightning thinned out. It could have been an hour. Perhaps more. Time stood still, no longer ticking with each second of the clock, but void of sound altogether as Vlad lost himself in the depths of his suffering.

She was gone.

*What was he to do now?*

Eventually, he rose, the warm air in the room becoming unbearable. He opened a window and let the cool air in. Moonlight painted the forest in silver. The same moon he'd stared at for hours dreading ever experiencing this feeling again. Pleading for company and praying if he ever got it, it wouldn't be ripped away. But this castle was his cage and he its prisoner like it had always been.

A cool breeze caressed his hair, carrying a sound. A string of curse words in a feminine voice.

His eyes snapped to Zar's.

Vlad grabbed the bat and moved faster than he'd ever moved, almost making himself nauseous. He appeared at the back gate, letting Balthazar go and staring at Lenore.

She was soaking wet, hair plastered to her face and holding an unlit lantern. Her boots and dress hem were covered in mud.

"Can you believe Marty went lame and I had to huff it all the way on foot?"

Vlad couldn't move. He couldn't believe she was here.

Lenore didn't seem to notice his stupor as she hiked her overstuffed pack higher on her shoulder. "Damn lantern went out and I've ruined my clothes." She sighed, finally looking at him. "I'm sorry I'm late. I—"

Vlad picked her up and spun her around, cutting off her words.

*She'd come back.*

"Vlad. I can't breathe."

He set her down. "Sorry. I just—" He smoothed back the hair from her rain slicked face. "You're here."

She frowned. "Of course I'm here. Albeit, quite late, but—" Lenore searched his eyes, her face dropping. "Were you worried I wouldn't come back?"

He couldn't stop the tiny sob that came out of him.

"Oh, Vlad." Lenore put his face in her hands and looked him square in the eyes. "I'm not going to abandon you."

He hugged her tight, refusing to let go until she peeled herself away, kissing him once more. She turned her attention on Balthazar. "Come here, you little furball."

Zar flew over and Lenore wrapped them all in a group hug. There were happy squeaks and tears of joy as they held onto one another, feeling more like a family than any of them had ever had.

Vlad slung her pack over his shoulder as they entered the castle with Balthazar close behind, anxious to get his claws on the peaches and strawberries she'd brought back for him.

Back in the Great Hall, Lenore told them all about her trip to Shademoss. They discussed her retrieving Marty in the coming days and planned a group visit to the town in the spring. She sat draped in Vlad's lap, his arms wrapped around her as she threw strawberry slices across the room to Balthazar who tried to catch them in his mouth.

The fire from the hearth provided light, but it was their loyalty and friendship that burned brightest. The Great Hall had seen gatherings of hundreds, but it was never full of as much warmth and laughter as it was between the three of them and the future they were planning—together.

# NEXT IN THE SERIES...

## Vlad and Friends: Move to Town

### Book II

Follow Vlad, Lenore, and Balthazar as they venture to the town of Shademoss, encountering exciting experiences and meeting new friends in the second book in this cozy Dracula-inspired series.

**Release date TBA**

# ACKNOWLEDGEMENTS

Thank you to everyone who has been there with me as this book has taken shape. Encouraging me when I stupidly decided I could tackle this project in four months from start to finish, talking through my story plot holes and problems with me, and showing their support for these characters.

Thank you to my writing group who yelled at me for being mean to Balthazar and said he should be protected at all costs. Your critiques and assistance in bringing this story to life have been immensely helpful, and the women in this group truly are a guiding light in my life.

To my TikTok friends who watch me write my stories online, thank you. I enjoy showing you the behind-the-scenes, chatting on livestreams, and showing you the progress as a new book goes from inspiration to a completed work. Thank you for your support and I hope I can continue to deliver stories that you enjoy.

## NICOLE HOLLAND

To my family, friends, and husband, thank you for being supportive of me since day one, in whatever it is I choose to take on. I have been blessed with wonderful people in my circle and am incredibly grateful I get to experience this life with all of them by my side.

I love you all.

# ABOUT THE AUTHOR

After a decade in the FBI, Nicole left the Bureau to work on creative pursuits. She lives in Texas where she enjoys tending to her gothic garden, getting bookish tattoos, and making videos on TikTok for both writers and readers.

# ALSO BY NICOLE HOLLAND

Other published works by Nicole Holland include:
Shadowbound
Rellington
Flame Vol. 1

Made in the USA
Coppell, TX
01 November 2025

62239953R00132